Daddy was uh Mobsta

Daddy was uh Mobsta
Copyright © 2014 by Robert Bowden.
Published 2014.

First edition published 2014.

Published in the United States by
Uaintgettinmy Publishing
3032 16th St. Suite 313
San Francisco, CA 94103−3403

Adobe® and Chaparral® are either registered trademarks or trademarks of Adobe Systems Incorporated in the United States and/or other countries.

Cover Design by Loren Kelly (REN)
Co−Edited by Susan Ragsdale and Janelle Murphy
Book Design: Barany Publishing

ISBN: 978−0−9815932−3−4

Printed in the United States of America.

Daddy was uh Mobsta

FLEETWOOD

Uaintgettinmy Publishing

San Francisco

This Book is Dedicated 2 My Father

(Rudolph Gentry Bowden)
aka
"Sonny"
Love you, Pops

ACKNOWLEDGEMENTS

There's no way I could have written this book without the help and encouragement of some key people at crucial times. To them I say, "Thanks for helping me and being there through all the phases of this project."

First of all, thank you, Jesus for your whoppings, direction, and your Grace and Mercy. Thank you so much to my comrades Mike Brown Director of Inner City Youth, and Sister Robin from P.I.C. who always sticks by me no matter what project I'm doing. Shout out to Juilette and Bonita for helping me with The Homeboyhotline. Much love and respect to Kevin Weston who taught me the art of writing. Peace to Davey D, you always show me love bruh. Hard knock Radio 4life, thanks to Rudy Corpuz, Bubba Hamp, Mister Banks, Marvelous Marv, Kevin Epps, Bernard from Alexander Bookstore, Sister Karen and Tomika, your whole family from Marcus Bookstore.

Peace to J.J., PamPam Djx−1, Kmaxx, KK Baby, Big Will and the whole staff at Kpoo for always supporting me. Peace to San Francisco Bayview for always supporting me. Paula Hendricks who gave me the game originally on how to self−publish a book. Much love and thanks to Susan Ragsdale who is the coolest supervisor ever and who helped edit my book. Ezra, my book designer on this book, thanks for being patient with me during the process, we got it done! And Loren Kelly (REN) from Dirty Mackin, my deep East Oakland homey, who did the graphics on *Bloodtest* and this book. I love y'all like a french fry love ketch up, for real.

CHAPTER 1

The light drizzle bounced steadily on beat off the window as the dark clouds rolled through the sky's night. Cars horns and the sound of their tires hitting the wet dirt road muffled the air, as people made their way home. The smell of wet cotton was the aroma and it crept into the cracked windows of the southern drivers. This was Buford, South Carolina; a country cotton picking town filled with hard working blacks who had built it and cared for the slave owners from past centuries, who still occupied the community. The racist white former plantation owners who were mad slavery was over and trying hard to still hold onto the ways of the past.

It was 1953 now though and things were supposed to be getting better for blacks in the south. Many owned their own homes now, even though modest and small, heated by wood stoves, and some still with outhouses. But it was theirs, finally somewhere to say this is my land. Most black folks had their own gardens and some livestock. Everything was homemade from the food to the clothing.

Tonight was a quiet Friday night inside the home of the Laneys. The walls of the home were all oak with the same wood on the hardwood floors, holding up an old refrigerator and a wooden stove used for heat and also to cook on. It has a few pictures that hung on the wall depicting former slave revolts, visuals of Nat Turner and Harriet Tubman. It has two beds in the single room with a table near the kitchen area and a throw rug in the middle of the floor that looked worn out but clean. This was paradise for a single black mother who had lost her husband 3 years prior to cancer and cleaned houses around town to make ends meet.

There she sat by the bed with her pregnant daughter sweating and begging for mercy with every breath. She was expecting a newborn at any moment now. Ms. Laney known to everyone as 'Granny' around town paced the floor frantically. This wasn't her first delivery of a child, but this time it was her daughter's baby, her grandchild, her first and things weren't going right. She knew something was wrong she just knew it.

"Just breathe slow, baby, and push. Push hard, baby, push. It's coming."

"Oh my lord. Please Jesus, help me. Please lord have mercy on me," Big Mama screams as she tried hard as she could to push the baby out. Granny nicknamed her daughter Big Mama at a young age due to her being so chubby. The name stuck throughout her childhood. Granny ran into the kitchen for more hot water and towels, as blood gushed out from between the legs of Big Mama.

"Oh Lord, please. Lord, please let this baby come out. Please lord!" Big Mama continued to beg.

"Hold on baby, here I come we going to make it thru this, Gods will! We will make it..! You just hold on child. Breathe in and out slowly baby and push hard."

"I'm pushing momma, but this is hurting! Please Lord, please help me!!" Big Mama let out a scream that could be heard throughout the county. Granny took the towels she had grabbed and begin trying to soak up the blood and fluids that were coming out of her daughter, praying at the same time.

"Hold on baby! Hold on! We almost there!" After cleaning away the blood Granny could see the baby's head.

"Please momma?! Please momma? Lord this hurts. Lord have mercy, Lord have mercy, please?!"

"Push, baby, push. I see the head. Push, baby child, push."

A loud knocking was coming from the front door.

"Who is it? My lord, knocking at my door like that."

"It's Irene. It's Irene. What's going on?" Irene was Granny's neighbor and friend for years having moved in at the same time in the house next door. She lived there with her husband and no kids she was unable to have kids from an accident in the fields she had where she and her husband worked picking cotton together. They lived a very quiet life.

"Come on in Irene and hurry up! Big Mama's having her baby hurry up. I need your help woman." Irene came bursting into the door. She almost went in shock when she look on the floor and saw all the blooded bandages.

"My God. What's wrong Granny, this girl is bleeding a lot?"

"I know, child. Please help me. The baby is coming out. Everything will be okay, just go get me more hot water and towels and quit standing there with your mouth open. Please hurry up, please."

"Oh my God, please help me, please," screamed Big Mama as more blood and fluids came rushing from between her legs. The baby started to emerged more from Big Mama as she continued to scream. In ran Irene with more towels and hot water.

"Here you go. Here you go, Granny."

"Thank you, thank you!"

"Push, Big Mama. Push, child!"

"I'm pushing!! I'm pushing!!"

"There you go. I see it. Here it comes, child. Here it comes," Granny said as the baby begin to come all the way out covered with blood and fluids from the mother.

"Irene, go get more cleanly towels. Hurry." Irene took off running, coming back within seconds.

"Here you go, Granny. Here you go."

Irene handed the towels to her, breathing hard, looking at the baby as Granny eased her out of the womb of Big Mama. Finally, she had a new born boy in her hands. A boy. Her grandson. She gave him a smack on the butt and he let out a big cry as she begin wiping the baby off.

"Big Mama, you did it gal. Look at your pretty baby boy you just brought into this world." As she look up she noticed Big Mama head leaned to the right and her eyes completely closed.

"Big Mama. Big Mama, is you okay child?" Granny screamed as she moved to the side of the bed and shook her, feeling for her pulse at the same time.

"Oh Lord, Irene, this gal done went into shock. Run, call the doctor and get your car. We got to get her to the hospital before we lose her. Hurry up, gal, hurry up."

Irene took off running out the door as fast as she could to her house. Granny finished wiping the child off and sat him in a cradle by the bed. She then ran into the kitchen and got a towel and ran some cold water on it. Running back into the front room, she placed it on her daughter head, rubbing her wrist and putting cold water on her forehead, squeezing it from her towel slowly letting it drip on her daughter neck.

"Lord, please, lord, please don't take my child. You just brought me a grandbaby. Please lord, don't take my only daughter. Please." Big Mama was her only child. A good girl, well−mannered, good in school. She had got pregnant by her first boyfriend, who had just went to the army and got killed on his first mission. They were supposed to be married when he got back from his duty. Now it was on granny to help raise her daughter and grandbaby. A loud blaring horn came from outside. It was Irene. She had pulled up in her car, an old beat up blue ford station wagon. The dust filled the air from the sudden stop on the country road.

"Here I come. Here I come. Let me get this gal up." Irene got out the car running and came into the house sweating.

"Let me get the baby in the car. I'll come back and help you with Big Mama," she said as she walked towards the bed with her arms out.

Granny with all her strength grabbed up Big Mama and practically drugged her across the room to the front door.

"Here let me help you. I got the baby in the car," said Irene as they put Big Mama in the back seat of the car. Granny got in the front and reached across the seat and continued to rub her daughters head and put cold water on her wrist trying to bring her outta shock. She pull the cloth down over the baby's head so see could keep an eye on her new grandson at the same time. As the car took off speeding down the dirt road headed to the local hospital.

"Please lord, please, let us makes it to the hospital, please."

After a mile of riding Granny looked back and saw yellow in her daughter's eyes then her eyes went in the back of her head.

"Oooooohhh no, lord. Ooooh no, lord, no," Granny screamed as she looked over the seat at her daughter. She knew she was gone. Irene pulled the car over on the side of the two lane road as far as she could. The daily traffic passed by being noisy slowing down trying to find out what was going on. Both Irene and Granny cried loudly. Granny snatched the front passenger door open and open the back door, grabbing Big Mama and shaking her, trying to force life back in her, giving her mouth to mouth, but it was too late. At the moment, Granny started shaking really hard like she was having a seizure. Irene realized she was going in shock behind all the events that were unraveling around her. Irene got out the car and ran around to the side Granny was at.

"Granny, you okay? You okay?" she asked her knowing she wasn't as she held her in her arms. Granny was shaking really hard. Irene look up and there staring at her were the biggest pretty brown eyes see had ever seen peeping from half way out behind a blanket. It was the little newborn boy.

"Little boy, you sure came into this world with a whole lot of excitement. You just stay quiet. I got to get your Granny to the hospital." Granny lay slumped under Big Mama. Irene reached over and closed Big Mama eyes, slammed the car door and ran around the car. She jumped in and took off smashing to the hospital barely missing oncoming traffic as she zigged zagged into traffic hoping to save her friend's life.

The hospital was a four story pale looking building needing paint. It resembles a big correctional camp from a view (actually, it was a former prison) with a large bare wired fence, removed now, surrounding the premises. It had one ambulance for the whole county which was now pulling in. After damn near running into the emergency room entrance door with the car, Irene finally got out of the car screaming. Nurses came out running frantically to the car and put both Big Mama and Granny on stretchers. After checking Big Mama vitals on the way in they realized she was dead and covered her up. Irene grabbed the baby out the cradle and a nurse came up to her and took him from her arms knowing Irene was unstable at the time. Finally, sitting in the waiting room with her legs trembling anticipating the news of her friend Granny, in walks the nurse.

"Hello, ma'am. My name is Nurse Smith. Unfortunately, I have some bad news."

"Oh my God, not Granny. Not Granny."

"No, ma'am. The older lady is resting. She'll be okay in a few days. She just went into shock, but unfortunately her daughter didn't make it. She passed on the way here. We couldn't revive her." Irene began crying and shaking even though she figured already that Big Mama was dead. Hearing it was terrible for her ears.

"So how's the baby? Where is the baby? Where is my nephew?" Irene said, already claiming the boy.

"He is fine. Doing what newborns do, crying and wanting to get fed."

"Can I see Granny and the baby please mama?"

"Yes. But Granny is still asleep."

"How long do you plan on keeping her here?"

"Like I said ma'am, we don't know exactly. Maybe two days."

"Well can I take the baby home with me?"

"I'm sorry ma'am. The child can only be released to immediate family."

"What do you mean? That's my nephew."

"Ma'am, I'm sorry. Doctor's orders from the county welfare. There's nothing I can do."

"I understand." Irene wiped away her tears and went into the room standing by the bed of her friend she had knew for the last 10 years. She bowed her head and prayed. Then she left out the hospital and headed home. It seemed like the days went by fast. There she was days later sitting there again in the hospital waiting room, waiting for Granny who had regained conscious and was ready to go home. After signing the birth certificate and taking full custody of him through some paperwork given to her by the county worker, she was finally ready to go home with her grandson. She had named him Rudy.

"Hey Granny, how you doing?" said Irene as Granny walked through the doors towards her.

"Irene, I just pray to God that he give me strength to make it through this."

"He will give you strength, Granny. He will. Come on let's go." She said, getting up from the seat reaching out to her.

"You know, this boy here, he done came to the world, and it changed my whole world. He gone change the world, Irene. I can see it in his eyes," she said as she look at the bundle of joy in her arms. Irene helped her friend by holding her arm, guiding her through the door into the car. After they got settled in the car, they pulled off the hospital grounds back onto the dirt road and headed down into the black section of town, what they knew as home. They rode in complete silence. Irene didn't really know what to say and she knew her friend was still dealing with so much so she just put her arm around her, and let the music play softly as they rode home.

CHAPTER 2

The new sound of baby chatter, baby talk, and lullabies from Rudy at night was the perfect combination for the healing Granny needed. The loss of her daughter was felt daily, but with Rudy there growing every day and Granny being a mother again, it became a new beginning not an ending. It seems like days ago when Rudy was crawling around the floor getting into everything he could, he was now 6 years old, and it was the beginning of the summer. The trees were bright green, complimenting the beautiful grass of the south. The air filled with the fresh smell of the spring harvest cotton. Kids played in the local water holes and parents planned for picnics and long walks at nights then retiring on their porches to reminisce.

On this particular day, Rudy was headed to his favorite spot, the water hole, for some fishing, which he loved more than anything because he got a chance to contribute to the household. Rudy had caught on quick with fishing lessons taught to him by Granny. He always came home with at least 10 to 12 fish every time making Granny blush at the accomplishments of her grandson. Rudy was a hardworking little man always wanting to help Granny around the house, even though he was only 6 years old. Since he was 3 and a half, he always swept the floor of the house and porch, took out the garbage, and helped Granny wash the dishes at night. He was a well−mannered little dude. That was one thing that was always said about Rudy from people around town. Also, he loved church−was there every on Sunday with Granny.

"Granny, is it okay if I go to the water hole and do some fishing? I finished sweeping. My chores are done, ma'am."

"Yes, baby, you can go. You just make sure that you back here on this porch fore it gets dark, you hear me?"

"Yes, ma'am, I hear you and thank you. I'll see you later. Love you Granny."

"Love you too, baby." Granny said as she watched her grandson run out the door with his fishing pole and tackle box in hand which he had made homemade from scratch. Every time she heard his voice she heard her daughter and felt her spirit. Granny knew Big Mama would be so proud of her child.

As Rudy made his way down the road the sound of the wind breezing through the trees could be heard along with the birds chirping and the scatter of squirrels climbing the long pine trees of the south. The walk to the water hole was Rudy's favorite part of the day he had a steady stride to the hole, at a young age you could tell he had confidence just by how he walked with pride and his head up, always looking you dead in the eyes when he spoke to you from his hard work around the house his little muscles were already forming a muscular frame. Granny use to catch him flexing in the mirror sometimes. As Rudy approached his normal spot by the water hole he noticed someone standing there already fishing it was a white kid, Rudy instantly got heated and walked up to him.

"Hey what's up? What's your name? Mine's is Rudy."

"My name is Zack."

"I never seen you before. Do you live round here?"

"Yup, we just moved down here from Virginia. Me, my moms, and dad."

"So this your first time coming here?"

"Saw it yesterday and came back today."

"This is where I fish everyday."

"Can we share it and fish together? We can split whatever we catch. I am a good fisherman."

Rudy thought for a moment feeling like for the first time in his life he was being challenge. Granny always told him don't start nothing with no one but always end it but be nice to people you never know who you will need in life, so after giving it some thought, he said, "You say you fish good huh? Well so do I and I know it's bunches of fishes in there so yup we can split what we catch and meet back every day after I do my chores."

"Okay do you have bait? Cause if not I have some."

Zack ran by the tree near the waterhole dug for a while then came up with a bag of worms. Rudy stood there in shock he had never seen someone do that before and most of the time he didn't use worms he used old bread but he was curious so he just watch Zack as he put the worm on his hook. Zack hand a custom rod, a pretty brown one with a fancy spin reel. Rudy was in love with it from the jump.

"Can I hold it when you finish? I never seen no fishing pole like that. Were you get that from?"

"My grandpa gave it to me before he died. See here's his name right here."

Zack was from a very abusive family. His mother was a hard working nurse and his father a former military man addicted to alcohol and beating his wife. Zack hated his father and vowed to one day kill him when he got bigger for all the times his mother cried and had black eyes. She was a pretty woman but his father never allowed her to go out and dress nice he was so scared she would run off, but the truth was Zack mother was very loyal to him, having been her only boyfriend in her life, and had paid for her college while he was in the service. He was a good man she always thought, it was what that damn war had done to him it had made him crazy and then left him to deal with the real world, so she stuck in there hoping and praying one day he would change.

After the boys baited their poles they begin their quest to see who could catch the most fish that day. Patiently waiting on a bite neither one said anything only working their own secrets anticipating the moment. Occasionally they looked over at each other, then right back to eyeing the rod and pole and water.

Then outta nowhere Zack rod began to jerk hard he had a bite.

"I got one. I got one, Rudy," Zack said excited.

"Reel him in slow. Dang, it look like a biggie. Zack, take your time. Don't lose him." As Zack reeled in the catch, he saw Rudy pole jerking. Rudy was watching Zack and not really paying attention to his pole.

"Rudy, look. You got one too. You got you one, look." Rudy looked over at his pole sticking out the ground and began to smile, deep inside he didn't want to be out done at his own fishing hole even though he wasn't mad at Zack for getting a bite first.

"I knew it was going to hit. I knew it. Zack, make sure you reel him in slow. I got this joker. I got'em."

Rudy picked up his reel and began slowly reeling in the fish. It was giving him resistance but for a youngster, Rudy handled his pole very well. As Rudy was reeling his in, Zack was taking off his first catch of the day smiling from ear to ear already placing him in his bucket and putting the bait on for the next catch. Rudy finally got his catch in as Zack was casting out again. All day they trade catches every time Rudy caught one, so did Zack.

"Zack, I think you my good luck charm. I never caught this many in one day."

"Me either. We a bad team, buddy. Rudy and Zack the best fisherman in the county." They both let out a big laugh and continued their fishing. At the end of the day they had caught almost 20 a piece. They both walked home smiling and laughing. Rudy knew Granny would be happy and Zack knew his moms would also be proud of him and he had made him a good friend. So for the next week every day they meet at noon by the water hole and continued their good fishing spree. On this one particular day when they were walking home Zack whole conversation changed.

"Rudy, do you think it would be okay if I came to your house for a little while till it gets dark? I don't feel like going home."

Rudy could tell the way his new friend said it something wrong. Even though Zack was one year older than Rudy he looked up to him.

"Yup that's okay. My Granny been wanting to meet you anyways."

As they walked home Zack told Rudy of how his dad had beat his moms up this morning before he left and how he didn't want to go home till he thought they were sleep and he told him how he was going to kill his dad one day. Rudy having never had to deal with something like that put his arm around Zack and told him everything would be okay.

"Just talk to granny. She will know what to do. She know everything. It's going to be okay. Don't worry. We the best fisherman in the county."

Zack smiled and they continued their walk.

"Hi, Granny. I'm home. I got some more fish for you and I brought Zack home with me," Rudy said as they walked thru the door. Granny looked up and smiled at her grandson. She was so proud of him.

"Rudy, go in the kitchen and bring the plate with the cloth over it. I got a surprise for you and Zack. I was going to save it for tomorrow, was bout to put in the oven but since you brought Zack home it's no time than the better. And bring that pitcher of lemonade with you."

Rudy made his way into the kitchen as Zack just stood there.

"Zack, come and sit down. Son let me take a good look at you. I done heard a lot about you. Feel like I already know you."

"Yes, mama."

"So how you doing today?"

"I'm okay I guess."

Granny could sense something was bothering him. "What's wrong son?"

"Nothing, really. Nothing."

"Zack, it's okay. You can talk to me, baby. Commere and sit beside Granny. I done heard so much about you, it feel like you my son too."

That eased the tension Zack was feeling, he sat down beside Granny.

"Granny, my dad gets drunk and beats up my momma. I don't like him. I wish I was big enough to kill him." Zack said it with a vicious tone.

"Son, don't ever say things like that because you don't mean it."

"Yup, I do. I hate him. I wish he was dead. All he do is beat my moms and get drunk."

"Well, baby, at night just get on your knees and pray for him. Ask GOD to help your daddy quit doing it."

"Do you think GOD will listen?"

"I know he will. He will always watch over you. Never forget that."

"What if my dad don't believe in GOD?"

"It don't matter. God will watch over you and your momma no matter what."

"Thank you, Granny, so much."

Zack leaned in and hugged her, as Rudy walked in the living room and sat down.

"Well the best fisherman in the county, it's time for y'all to start making some money."

They both sat up and smiled listening attentively.

"How, Granny, how?" they both said at the same time.

"Well, hand me that plate."

Rudy passed the plate to Granny.

"Rudy, go get two empty jars for you all lemonade."

Rudy ran out the room back in seconds with the two jars.

"Here you go, Granny."

"Pour you and Zack a full jar. I already had some."

"So how we going to make some money, Granny?" Rudy asked.

Granny unwrapped the plate and handed Rudy and Zack two big fish sandwiches.

"Here take a bite of these and tell me what you think."

Both the boys dug into the sandwiches head first.

"Man, Granny, these are great," said Rudy.

"Yup this the best fish sandwiches I ever had," said Zack.

"Okay so this the plan. Y'all going to have a fish sandwich and drink stand. I already cleaned all the fish you all brought in for the last few weeks. You all have enough fish to last for at least a month."

"How much should we sell them for, granny, a piece?"

"Yeah how much?"

"Well, I was thinking like 50 cent a piece and 25 cent for a cup of the homemade lemonade. Y'all should easy make a hundred dollars a week."

"Man, I can buy me some new shoes and pants for school and a coat," said Rudy.

"Yeah me too but we only got like one month till school start."

"Well if you all work very hard you all will be okay. What you all need to do is go out in the back and build you a stand outta that wood back there and it's some old wheels from a cart your grandfather had back their also. You can take the wheels off of that so it will roll."

"I know how to build stuff good," Zack said.

"Well what you all two fisherman waiting on?"

Both the boys took off out the front door and headed for the back. Within hours, they were standing in front of their new fish sandwich stand on wheels they had built. Granny came out the house with two fresh jars of lemonade. She had been watching them out the back window of the house the whole time.

"Here you go. Look like you all need this here."

"Thank you so much, Granny."

"Yes mama, thank you," Zack said.

★★★★★

Three weeks had passed now and the small fish sandwich stand was the talk of the town. People couldn't believe how these two boys had their own sidewalk restaurant and how good the sandwiches were, many a days the boys ran out and had to shut down the stand. Within those three weeks Zack and Rudy both had saved up $125.00 a piece. The boys had made a vow to give Granny the money from the last week for all she had done the cooking and the idea. In between the stand the boys had a usual routine get up early do their chores at home and meet at Rudy's house get the stand sell sandwiches and then go to the water hole to fish again. On this particular day the boys were just finishing up their fishing when some older kids appeared outta nowhere; three large white boys looking like they were in high school.

"Say boy, you little nigger lover, what the hell are you doing?" one of them said talking to Zack.

Zack was surprised he spun around with his mouth open. Rudy, knowing the ways of the south, knew it was about to be trouble so he slid his hand into his pocket to get his buck knife, the one he used to sometimes get the fish off the hook when they were stuck.

"He's fishing with me what you want with him?" Rudy said to them dropping his bucket in his other hand. Zack eased back from them as they walked closer and put his hand on his buck knife in his back pocket.

"Look here, little nigger you and your nigger lover buddy been making my money. It's time for you to pay up."

"We don't owe you nothing," Zack said full of confidence now with his hand on his knife and seeing that his friend Rudy wasn't backing down.

"Yeah we don't owe you nothing. We sell what we catch. This our spot."

"Nigger, this our town you black muthafucka."

"From now own you work for us," said the biggest kid of the bunch as he walked towards Rudy.

Rudy knew it was now are never so he lunged towards the older kid with the knife in hand stabbing him in the arm which he kept doing it repeatedly.

"He stabbed me. He stabbed me. The fucking nigger stabbed me!" the big kid said laying on the ground as the blood gushed from his arm. His buddies saw the blood and took off running up the road. Zack came over and began kicking the kid in the head where he had fell to the ground holding his arm.

"You son ova bitch. You son ova bitch. This our stuff, you son ova bitch. You aren't taking our stuff you son ova bitch." Zack had snapped. Rudy saw it in his eyes. He had kicked the boy damn near unconscious. Rudy grabbed his friend and saw a look in his buddy eyes he had never seen before.

"Zack, we got'um. Zack! Zack, you gonna kill'um," Rudy screamed as he pulled his friend off the kid.

"Fucking punk ass red neck," Zack said as he kicked the kid once again in the head.

"Dang, Zack. You a wild man."

"Ain't nobody gonna mess with us. We don't mess with no one and you the only friend I got. No one messing with us, no one Rudy. Never. I mean that."

Rudy put his arm around him looking back at the kid on the ground. He knew then he had a friend for life as they walked away laughing at the kid on the ground and at his friends who they saw hiding behind a tree watching. That day the boys felt extra good they had hailed their own against the bullies of the county.

"You know what, Rudy? Let's go hunting tomorrow."

"Hunting? Hunting what?"

"Rabbits and squirrels. My dad taught me how to shot when I was just three. I got two rifles at home with good aim. My mom's said it going to get cold soon and the fish will be hard to catch and people want come out that much so she said we should hunt for rabbits and squirrels skin them and sell them to people house to house to cook. What you think about that?"

"Zack, I don't know how to hunt. I never did it before. I don't even know how to shoot a gun."

"I'll teach you, Rudy. I know you'll be good. I can tell."

"Yeah, how's that?"

"By the way you stabbed that punk with the knife. You sneaky, Rudy, you sneaky."

They both looked at each other and grinned.

"Well let me talk to Granny bout it when I get home and I will let you know tomorrow okay?"

"Okay."

"Don't you need me to walk with you home Zack? They might try something."

"If they come back, I got something for them." Zack pulled out his buck knife he had in his back pocket. They both started laughing and slapped hands.

"Okay, sees you tomorrow then, Zack."

"See you tomorrow, Rudy."

When Rudy got home he told Granny what had happen and she told him be careful and never start nothing with no one, but don't take no mess from no one either and gave him a hug. Then he asked her if he could go hunting with Zack. At first Granny said no but she thought about it and agreed to let him hunt. She just told him to be careful while they were in them woods with them guns which Zack was going to provide.

★★★★★

Early that next morning with the sun just coming up over the pine trees of the south and dew on the ground the wind blew slightly, it was a pretty morning in the south Rudy and Granny talked the whole way as they walked and the morning traffic passed by them leaving a cloud of dust. Granny she had on a hat with a scarf tied around it so she gave it to Rudy to cover his mouth when the cars passed by. Rudy and Granny, they were on their way to the local market unable to afford a car just yet and Ms. Irene was already gone for work so they walked to the store to get more flour and cornmeal. It was the only store in town that allowed blacks to come in there to shop were the whites shop, but only during certain hours. They had a racist security guard who worked there who always gave blacks a hard time when they came. As Rudy and Granny made their way around the store looking for what they came to get, they noticed him following them.

"Rudy pay that rascal no mind." Granny noticed how he was irritating Rudy.

"Why do he think we going to steal something Granny? We got money."

"That's just how some people are, baby. Evil got the devil in them."

Rudy looked up at Granny and shook his head.

"Rudy, grab me a roast outta there. It's on sale we might as well get it now."

"Okay, Granny." Rudy walked over and got the roast and headed back to Granny looking around for the racist guard who had disappeared from their sight.

"Here you go, Granny," Rudy said and he placed the roast in the basket.

"Thank you, baby. You the best fisherman and grandson in the south."

That made Rudy smile. Granny was his heart and soul. He loved her to death. In his mind he told his self—one day you aren't going to have to work for no one no more.

"You know what, Rudy? I think I'm going to wait till next week and cook that roast. You can take it back, Rudy." So Rudy grabbed the roast and put it back, then came back to Granny who had made it to the line, outta nowhere the guard walks up to them.

"What did y'all niggers do with that roast?"

Granny spun around and looked at the man shocked by his harsh demeanor even though she knew he was racist she knew they had did nothing wrong.

"Excuse me, sir. My grandson put it back. We decided not to buy it today."

"That's a damn lie. I saw you put it in your purse, nigger bitch. Open that purse."

At the same moment the word came outta his mouth, Rudy reached in his pocket with his hand on his knife and was about to lunge at the guard.

"Rudy, Rudy, Rudy, no. No." Granny knew what was about to happen. She knew her grandson wasn't going to allow no one to disrespect her ever.

"Open your damn purse, nigger, or go to jail."

Granny knew she couldn't win so she open her purse then the guard snatched it out her hand and dump everything on the floor. Rudy stood there swelling in anger watching the guard.

"Well, I be damn. It isn't here picked that shit off my floor before I put you outta here," he said.

Rudy bend down and got all of Granny's possessions off the floor and put them in her purse. Granny watched Rudy. She knew he was thinking about doing something.

"Baby, don't worry about it. Long as you know that you did nothing don't worry about it. GOD will always watch over us." Granny paid for her stuff and they walked out. As they walked home it was a strange silence. Rudy just carried the bags not saying nothing almost getting hit by a car.

"Boy, watch out! Keep your eyes on the road. These people can't drive at times."

"Sorry, Granny."

"Rudy, I know what that man did wasn't right and the way this world is isn't right but like I keep telling you always remember GOD will watch over us always."

"Yes ma'am."

They continued to walk.

"Granny?"

"Yes, son?"

"Did he do that because he got that uniform on?"

"It isn't the uniform. It's the person inside of it, baby. All them aren't bad, Rudy. Just most of them."

"Well, one day, I am going to get me one of them uniforms."

Granny noticed the change in his voice Rudy was crying but it was mad tears running down his face. Deep in his mind he made a decision to get a uniform like these racist people and repay them for all they had done to him and the people he had seen them mistreated.

"Yup, Granny. I am going gets me one, one day. Watch."

She looked down at her grandson, wiping his tears away and for some reason she knew he meant what he said and had his own secret plan for them.

CHAPTER 3

A two story old fashion red brick building sat inside a circle of tall pine trees. It had four large white columns in the front and a large shiny pole that held the American flag at the top. The lawn was manicured along with the shrubbery that lined up the dirt road entrance way to the school, the sound of children chatter could be heard throughout the facility.

The average day for the boys was spent walking to school together in their brand new clothes they had brought. The conversation usually contained making fun of the girls. They had yet to get to the age of liking them so girls was like not on their priority list. The boy's thoughts were focused on getting good grades so they could go hunting after school, even though Zack was seven years old, one year older than Rudy who was six, they both were in the same class because first through third grade were taught together because of the small community in Buford.

"Rudy, could you please stand up and give me the answer to the question, please?"

"Yes, ma'am."

"The answer is five. Two plus three is five."

"Good job, Rudy."

"Zack, could you please answer the next question?"

"Yes, ma'am. The answer is eleven. Six plus five is eleven."

"That is correct, Zack. You also did a good job."

"Thank you, ma'am."

The boys looked at each other and smiled. They knew they were the star pupils of the class, always getting good marks. The teachers really like them both and always told them they were special. After their hunting Rudy and Zack would spend time at Rudy's house studying hard then would have Granny go over their homework with some milk and cookies. Zack's father complained about him being at Rudy's house so much but he saw the happiness in his son when he wasn't drunk so he didn't put up too much fuss about it.

This continued for the next eight years. The boys were growing up fast, the stars of the local football and basketball team and also were the talk of the town being the salt and pepper team. They made more money hustling sometimes than the adults in the county.

It was getting close to sundown as the sky darkens slightly with every moment that past and the chill came into the air with a breeze, the boys kicked back by a tree in the woods with two jars of Granny famous lemonade sipping slowly taking a break the daily hunt had gone well.

"You know what, Rudy? I been thinking I want to go to the Air Force like my uncle did. He lives in California. He was a pilot. He flew all over the United States shooting down planes for the US Air Force now he kicking back taking it easy living the easy life outside of Oakland. I went out there when I was little one day. I am going to move out there. I bet you would like it. You should think about joining the Air Force too and coming with me."

"Man, they give you a uniform huh, Zack?"

"Yup. You can finally get your uniform you been talking about for all these years. Not a police uniform but it's still a uniform."

"That's good enough for me for now. I will ask Granny tonight if I can do it."

"Let's go, Rudy. It's getting dark. I got to get home soon."

"Okay, let's go."

The boys picked up their rifles and the catch for the day and headed home.

Rudy walked into the house excited and noticed Granny relaxing on the couch.

"Hey, Granny. What you doing pretty lady? How was your day?" He noticed her reading a letter. "What's that? Who is that from Granny?"

"It's a letter from your auntie May in Greensboro. She is terribly sick and can't handle that cousin of yours, Rico, I always told you about."

"Did he get in some more trouble?"

"No, not that I know of, but she asked me if I can let him come and stay with us for a while."

"So you going to let him, Granny? You going to let him come?"

"Son, to be honest with you, I really don't have no choice but if I did I wouldn't. That boy is hard headed and hot tempered.'

"Well maybe the country life will be good for him."

"Son, Greensboro isn't a big city like New York."

"Yeah, I know, but it's bigger than here, Granny. They got an airport and everything, Granny."

"And they got drugs and crime there too. People always getting shot up there. That boy Rico keeps a gun."

"For real? What kind?"

"Listen boy." Granny raises up from the couch and raised her finger at Rudy something she rarely did. "Don't let that young'un get you in no trouble. You and Zack doing real good on you all on your way to college. Don't let him mess your mind up with that foolish. You hear me?"

"Yes ma'am." Deep in his head Rudy couldn't wait for Rico to come. He had heard so much about his hustling gangster cousin. He wanted him to teach him everything so he would be ready for his revenge on every uniform there was out there.

"Baby, Imah go next door and use Ms. Irene phone and call up to Greensboro and talk with May. I'll be back in a in a bit. Your supper is on the stove."

"Thank you, Granny. Is there something you need me to do?"

"No. You just think about what I said bout that boy. You hear me, Rudy?"

"Yes, ma'am."

★★★★★

Days later at a filling station with dust flying everywhere, from the dirt road the cars left behind, when they pulled off, sitting there on a bench out in front wiping the sweat away and swatting flies was Granny and Rudy, waiting on cousin Rico's bus to pull in.

"Granny, I think that's it right there."

"It's bout dang time. I'm hotter one of them fast tail gals in church, boy."

"Ooooh, Granny," Rudy said half laughing he always loved how Granny put things. The big gray bus with foggy windows came to a stop little by little people piled off. Coming down the steps with a pimp limp was an extra dark skin boy with a big afro, big smile and glasses wearing a white t–shirt, jeans and boots.

"Hey, auntie, how you doing?" Rico said half jogging to Granny and hugging her. Rudy stood back sizing him up. He knew it was his cousin Rico. He wasn't taller than Rudy, but he was more muscular a complexion lighter with a thin scar on his right cheek. They looked like they were the same age with Rico's baby face but actually Rico was 5 years older than Rudy.

"I'm alright, baby. I'm alright just hot. We been waiting for a while. Rico this is your cousin, Rudy. Big mama's boy."

"What up, Cuz? Big Mama always treated me nice. I loved her and still do. She was a good lady."

"Thanks. My moms I heard was really special." They pause for a moment look at each other.

"Let me go over here and get my bags." Rico walked over to the driver and got his stuff then came back and they started walking down the road.

"So what's to do round here, Cuz?"

"Me and my buddy Zack, we hunt and fish and sell it at our sandwich shop."

"Yeah my mom's been telling how you was down here hustling, Cuz. I likes that. I'm a hustler, also."

"Do you like to hunt?"

"Well I can't say I ever shot a rabbit or caught a fish, but I do like to shoot guns, Cuzn." Rico started laughing.

"Listen here, boy. I'm telling you now, I am not having none of that foolish with you down here and I mean it. You hear me, Rico?" Granny exclaimed.

"Yes, ma'am. Yes, ma'am." Rico looked at Granny eye to eye but something in her told her it won't be long before he would be biting his words breaking his promise to be good.

They finally made it to the house. Zack came over and they went out hunting.

"Damn Zack, that's a bad rifle man."

"Yup thank you, but Rudy, he like the old one."

"It shoots better than that new one and its lighter, Cuz. That's why."

"Can I shoot it once?"

"There is not nothing moving out there."

"Fuck it. I just want to shoot it."

Rudy noticed how Zack's face changed with the sound of the bad words Rico used. It was really the first time the boys were around a young person who cursed like that. Neither of them said nothing, but they knew Rico was way ahead of them both when it came to the street life.

"My homeys in the boro got 38's for them fools who think they can take our shit."

"What stuff you talking bout?"

"Our reefer, our weed. I know yawl got some down here."

"Yeah them boys down the road be doing that, but we don't mess with that stuff. They just sent two of them to reform school. We play football and hunt and stay outta trouble."

"Down the road huh? We might have to see what they doing," Rico said laughing and grabbing the gun Zack was handing him at the same time. "Let me see that thing Zack."

Quickly Rico loaded the chamber aimed it towards the air and let off round after round after loading with a swift fierce motion.

"Dang. I have never seen anyone do a rifle like that."

"Yeah I learned a lot shit watching the cowboy movies. Especially the rifleman, I like him."

"I thought you said you never hunt before?"

"Not for no rabbits. I hunt for robbers before though."

"So you all about ready?"

"Yup let's take off, Rudy." Zack started leading the way through the tall pine wood trees with the wild brushes and familiar paths using his machete to chop his way through the woods and trying to spot anything moving.

"Hold up, be quiet," said Rico. Everyone stopped immediately.

"Look right there. There go a rabbit," said Rudy.

Rudy put his rifle on his shoulder and squeezed slowly and sound exploded from the gun with the rabbit falling at the same time.

"Bulls—eye! Shitted first fucking shot. That was pretty good. Good dang shot, Cuzn," Rico said.

"I think it was luck," Zack said laughing. Deep inside Zack wanted to show off Rico with the guns. He always thought he was the best gunman and plus he didn't want Rudy to feel it couldn't handle his back if he needed him. The boys continued to walk thru the woods plucking off rabbits and squirrels. The day was going.

"Hey, come mere, come mere," Rico said.

Rudy and Zack came over to were Rico was kneeling down in the brushes at.

"You all see what I see over there?"

Rudy looked to were Rico was pointing at and so did Zack. They both knew what they were looking at. They knew where they were at.

"That's reefer plants over there look like thousands of them, Cuzn. We rich. We bout to get rich, Cuzn."

"Rich. That isn't our stuff."

"Shit, we found it. It's ours now."

"What we gon do with it though? How we gon get rich with it?"

"Look Cuzn if that's what I think it is all we got to do is get that shit and get it to Greensboro and we going to be rich. You hear me? Let's go."

Rico took off running towards the reefer field. Zack took off right behind him followed by Rudy. After a few minutes jumping over shrubbery and ducking branches and limbs, the boys stopped. They were standing right at the bottom of the field.

"Look, there go somebody moving down there."

"Let me see," said Zack.

"It looks like the boys who tried to take our money. That is them punks."

"Fuck'em. Whoever they are, nothings about to stop us from getting that reefer. We can feed the family a long time off that, Cuzn. You here me?" Rico grabbed Rudy's jacket and looked at him dead in the eye. Rudy jerked his jacket away. He never liked no one grabbing or touching him. If it wasn't for him knowing it was Rico he would have punched him.

"We just got to do it right, that's all. And don't be grabbing on me, Cuzn. Never," said Rudy.

Zack looked at his friend. He wasn't surprised Rudy was with it. They both always talked of getting their families' outta there however it took.

"Let's us wait around for a while and see how many there are," Zack said.

"I'm go over there, Rico. You take the other side but don't crossfire. Signal with your shirt when you get were you at, okay, Cuzn? We ain't trying to shoot each other."

"Cuzn, I got you." Rico took off through the woods to the left and Rudy went to the right. Zack stayed where he was. After an hour they came back to the original spot.

"It's only three that I see," Rudy said.

"An old man keeps going in the shack coming in and out in with big bags on a cart."

"So that means it's four of them. That old man probably they dad or something. It don't matter," Rico said.

"The shack were they gotta be storing the reefer."

"We need a closer look."

"Just keep them guns up. You know they got some weapons."

"I been waiting to shoot them punks since that day they messed with us anyway," Zack said.

"Let's go."

The boys crept into the grounds of the place. It was a farm house with a big shack in the back, fields of green plants surrounded the wooden buildings. They could hear idle chatter in the house. The boys kept their guns high and moved around the property unnoticed.

"It's unlocked."

"Come on."

"'Imah stay here to make sure no one come behind y'all," Zack said.

Rico and Rudy walked into the shack, guns high, slowly. Rico slowed down even more.

"Damn. Good lord, damn," he said looking up in there air. It was racks and racks of sacks full of reefer stack neatly on shelves. Had to be over 500 of them and Rico was doing the math fast. It had to be 20 pounds in each sack. That was alotta money.

"Cuzn, we bout to feed the family. Let's go." Rudy kept his gun in the air looking around panning the place like a bank camera. He was looking for anything that could happen to stop them from getting outta there.

"We gonna come back. I gotta call my boy in Greensboro when we get back to the house. Let's go, Zack." Rico walked out the shack slowly with guns in the air still hearing the chatter from the house. Sounded like they were having a drunken dinner. In his head Rico thought it's time for us to eat. I been waiting on this damn. I'm glad I came down here. Back at Granny house the boys had put their catch up and were sitting on the porch.

"Rudy, you think I can use them peoples phone next door?"

"I don't know if they home."

"I need to call to Greensboro right quick." Rudy started walking towards Ms. Irene house.

"Come on, let's go see."

The boys followed Rudy, all of them caught in their own thoughts. Rudy was thinking, My Granny done worked hard enough I'm make sure Granny can relax when we get this money.

Zack was thinking bout how far away he could send his moms from his dad. Send her on a trip around the world, all expenses paid like a superstar, for all she had been through.

"Come on in."

"Ms. Irene, is it okay if my cousin Rico uses the phone to call to Greensboro?"

"Yeah child comes on in the phone over there. What Granny doing?"

"She by the stove mixing some stew I think."

"Well tell her I said hi when you get back."

"Yes, ma'am and thank you."

"You welcome son. just make sure you close that door when you leave."

"Okay."

Rico grabbed the phone and began dialing numbers then hesitated for a minute.

"Hello? Hello, Red? Red?" He was a older friend of Rico's who had just got outta reform school with his buddy lil Johnny for robbery.

"What's up? Who this?"

"This Rico, boy."

"What's up?"

"I told you were I was going, right? Well I found a field of reefer down here. I need you to get lil Johnny bout 4 pistols and get on the road tonight and be here in the morning. We'll be rich by the end of the week."

"You playing, boy."

"Now you know I don't play."

"Damn. It's that much reefer?"

"Hell yeah. Look, I'm on this lady phone next door I can't stay on here too long. You with it or not?"

"Hell yeah, I'm with it."

"Well, listen call me when you get here. Go get, here call me at this number. It shouldn't take you no more than 6 hours to get here. Make sure them guns put up good and get the biggest truck you can get from your uncle."

"I got you Rico, boy. You always coming up on something."

"Yeah well this one is gonna let us sit back after this."

"What bout the owners?"

"Fuck'um. What you think them guns for?"

★★★★★

Three days later at the edge of the field in the pitch black dark sat Zack, Rudy and Rico.

Red and lil Johnny were down the road in separate trucks waiting on the word from Rico. They each had walkie talkies Red had came up with in Greensboro.

"Yo, the lights just went out. We going in. Stay ready."

"Got you," replied Red.

"Let's move, Cuzn." Rico began creeping onto the property with his two 38's up in the air, his eyes open wide at a low cradled position, swiftly moving across the land to the barn with Rudy and Zack trailing him. Finally at the door Rico put one gun in his waist and removed the bolt cutters from the back of his waist and cut the chain and lock that was on the barn door.

"'Come on."

Rico open the door slightly put the bolt cutters back in his back and pulled out a flashlight, flicked it on looked up and saw all the sacks of reefer stack so neatly he looked over at Rudy and smiled.

"Call them. Let's get this done."

"Yo, come on in. I'm coming out. Start the trucks then turn them off and then coast on in."

"I got you."

Red started up the trucks put it in gear and then rolled off. He saw the entrance to the property and cut the engine. Rico, Rudy, and Zack were coming up to meet the trucks guiding them in, guns in the air. Everything was going good.

"Swing it around and put the back of the truck to the door," Rico told Red then ran to Lil Johnny's truck and told him the same thang.

With everything in position, it was like a machine, the way they loaded the reefer from those shelves. Within a few hours the trucks were packed and ready.

"The lights still out. I haven't seen no movement at all its quiet." Zack stood at the entrance to the barn with his rifle in hand pointed at the house that was dark.

"Let's go. We finished," Rico responded.

"We walking the trucks out to the road."

"Fuck that. Started'um up. Let's go."

The engines of the trucks started up and began rolling off the property. Rudy just knew the lights were going to come on in the house but they never did. They rolled straight off the property onto the road, and they were gone. They drove the trucks all the way back to Greensboro. Rudy and Zack rode along.

Three days later they had people coming from far as Virginia and Tennessee to get the cheapest pounds in the south after unloading the trucks when they got back they counted out 700 sacks of reefer. When they weighted them to pounds it was 2,500 pounds.

A few months later

"Boy, I love you, Cuzn. You the best thang ever happen in my life, coming to Buford. Shit, I love that place." Rico sitting back in the living room on the couch with a wad of cash in his hand, 38 on his lap, sipping on some good whiskey on ice with his feet up at his brick house by the lake he had brought deep in the woods. He had about 50 trained dogs roaming round the yard that would kill on sight. Rico had become the godfather of the city. He was running shit and he knew it and everyone else did too.

"Man, this what life about, Cuzn. All you need is money in the racist world and you will be okay," Rudy said cause at the tender age of 16 him and his crew were living good.

"You damn right about that," said Zack.

The months passed right along with the reefer. Before they knew it, it was all gone and they had money to burn living like kings in the south. Rudy and Zack had opened up their own store called Granny's in her name in Buford with a food counter for their sandwiches which Granny ran with her friends. Everyone was happy. Zack brought his parents a new home and his pops was going to AA meetings now. At least it was a start.

The boys were spending a typical weekend up in Greensboro chilling at Rico house talking shit.

"You know what I been thinking? I'm move to California with my uncle. I'm getting outta here," Zack said.

"I'm going with you, me and Granny. When we leaving?" said Rudy.

"I'm serious. I'm thinking bout leaving the end of the month. I called my uncle the other day he said when I'm ready, call him."

"I'm serious. too. But what we pose to do with the store?"

"Ms. Irene can run it."

"It's gonna be hard to talk Granny into leaving, you know that."

CHAPTER 4

Two days later sitting in the living room with Granny watching TV.

"Granny, what you think about moving to California?"

"What? What you say, boy? Is you done gone crazy? I ain't moving to no California. I don't care how rich Zack uncle is." Zack and Rudy had told Granny Zack's uncle had come into alotta money from oil and had gave Zack his favorite nephew enough to live for the rest of his life and a loan to open the store and he had loaned Rudy money to buy Granny her house.

"Why not? It's nice out there. We can move your store out there, have two of them. What you say?"

"No, boy. I'm not leaving my home. We just got this house what would I do out there?"

It was a loud knock at the door. It was Zack, breathing hard, as he opened the door, coming in.

"Hey Granny. Rudy you seen the news on TV? You seen the news?" Zack was sweating walking towards Rudy.

"What's wrong with you?"

"Turn the news on. Turn the news on."

Rudy got up and turn the channel to the local news there it was a big picture of Rico saying "cop killer" and under it "arrested for murder."

41

"My lord. What is going on?" Granny said. "Rudy turn that thang up. Turn it up."

"Today at 10:30am the police pulled over this young Greensboro man, Rico Jones, with two passengers in the car, for speeding. As the officers came to the car gun fire emerged out of the driver's window then out of the passenger side. One of the passengers in the car was killed along with one of the officers. The driver Rico Jones is still alive along with a man by the name of Johnny Reynolds. They both are in the county jail tonight. It's being reported that this young man and his friends were major marijuana dealers in the community. More details at 6 o' clock.

"Lord, have mercy. Lord, have mercy."

"Rudy, I don't want you back up there. Don't you go back up there."

It was a knock at the door.

"It's Irene," the voice said as the knob begin to twist. She was trying to come in but the door was locked.

"Hold on, Ms. Irene. Here I come," Rudy said never hearing the cars pulling up. It was the police. They were jumping outta their cars running towards the house finally reaching the door right as Rudy opened it knocking Ms. Irene down.

Zack took his gun from out his belt. Granny looked and gasped for air.

"Zack, no, no," Rudy said as he slid his gun out and slid it under the couch then Zack hid his at the same time. In came the police barging in with guns pointed in Rudy's face.

"Get on the fucking ground you nigger 'fore I kill your ass."

"My lord, what is going on? What is going on?" Granny said in shock.

"Shut the fuck up and you get on the ground too old bitch."

Rudy looked up and begin to move in the direction of Granny.

"Move again and Imah kill you nigger."

"The house is clear, sir," an officer said coming from the back room.

"What is going on? What is going on?" Granny said as Ms. Irene came in and sat beside her.

"Well, your boy and his nigger loving friend been selling reefer in Greensboro, North Carolina and your nephew up there done killed a police. His lil buddy up there telling it all. You won't be seeing these boys for a long time, old lady."

Granny begin crying as the police grabbed the boys, handcuffed them up, and lead them out the door into the police cars. They were off to Greensboro in the back seat, squashed in between two fat officers, with three police cars following them.

"Irene, Irene," Granny said rocking back and forth.

"Yeah."

"The police done got my boy and Zack. That nephew of mines done killed a police in Greensboro. I wish that Rico would have never come down here."

"So that's where them boys got that money, huh?"

"They was hustling/"

"Making big money. They always was working hard together, him and Zack. They ain't no bad boys, though, I know that they ain't."

"Yeah it was that Rico. Probably showed them all that mess."

"Well, they did do what they did but they help they families. I can say that."

"You dang right. And that's my baby. That's why I ain't bout to let them whites folks send my boy away like that. Irene hand me that phone over there."

Ms. Irene handed Granny the phone she dialed a few numbers.

"Hello? Hello?"

★★★★★

Sitting across the street from Granny's house while everything was going down the whole time was the racist security guard from the store that day. Now he was a sergeant in the local police department, known as Sergeant Smith. He was sitting there with two other men, his cousins. They just happen to be the ones who had got their reefer stole a few months earlier. They were ready to kill Rudy and Zack.

"I knew it was those fucking two niggers who did. Gosh darn it sum bitches. I knew it," said one of them.

"We should shoot they coon ass right here now," the other one said raising his gun up.

"Now, now, hold your beeches up. Wait a fucking minute. How will we get our money and reefers back first? We gots find out where it is."

"That old black bitch knows where it is. I bet you or that nigger loving boy's momma. One of them knows."

"I know one dang thing. They ain't living this fucking good off no fucking fish sandwiches."

"I'm keep a trail on these fuckers like a hound dog wit a fresh scent. Y'all just take it easy. We can get more reefers. Until then just take it easy for now I promise you, I'm get these black sum of bitches." Their car pulled off as the boys were lead out the house never knowing they were being watched and plotted on. Back inside Granny's house. She sat there holding the phone frantically.

"Why you ain't called down here and told me what's going on?"

"I just walked in the house." May had just got out the hospital three days prior.

"I just founded out sister. I don't know what to say. I'm in shock right now."

"Well they got Zack and Rudy in police cars on their way up there. All we can do is pray and get them boys some lawyers quick."

"How we gon pay for it?"

"Don't worry about that. I need you to find who the best lawyer up there and call me back. I wanna have a lawyer waiting on them when they get up there."

"Okay, okay."

"Call me right back as soon as you find out, May."

"Sister?"

"Yes, what's is it?"

"I'm sorry. I didn't mean to bring this in your life."

"Listen, we family, don't worry bout it. Find a lawyer."

Deep inside Granny was mad at her little sister for calling her and asking her to take care of that boy but it wasn't the time to tell her that.

★★★★★

Seven hours later at the downtown precinct sat Rudy and Zack handcuffed to a bench. Their lawyer Mr. Rilestien was in the office talking to the police trying to get their charges dropped but they had a signed confession from lil Johnny who was now sitting in a cell in protective custody.

"Here he come, Rudy."

Rudy opened his eyes as the lawyer walked out of the office towards them.

"Well, fellows, y'all gonna have to stay for a while. They won't set a bail but the evidence they do have is weak implicating you in the operation. Even with the signed statement I can breakdown their witness credibility so if y'all be patient, keep your mouths shut, in a couple of months I can get you in court and maybe get this dropped or you some probation."

"A couple of months?"

"Listen, what would it cost us to disappear?"

"What do you mean disappear?"

"Like you said, all they got is his word. If we make sure we never be seen in this county again and take care of who needs to be, get us a deal were we can go in the military immediately. Disappear. We ain't did shit."

The lawyer looked at Rudy. So did Zack, like where did he come up with that brilliant idea, hoping they would go for it.

"I'll be right back," the lawyer said walking away. He saw money signs money for him and the crooked police chief.

Rudy stay silent as he watched the lawyer make conversation with the police chief through the binds after. About fifteen minutes out walk the lawyer.

"You got a ten thousand dollars, you got a deal." Actually the lawyer was scamming. He only told the police chief he was going to get him five thousand. The other five thousand was for him.

"Get me to a phone."

The lawyer walked over to the s police sitting behind the desk.

"Excuse me, Officer, would it be alright if my client uses the telephone?" The officer looked up then over to the chief's window who was standing there watching every move. He nodded, so the officer got up and unhandcuffed Rudy.

"Granny, hey you alright?"

"Hey baby. Yeah I'm alright. Where you at?"

"They got us at this police station. Listen I need you to go to the bank and have Mr. Weiss give you the key to my safe deposit box. Take out 10,000 dollars and give it to my lawyer."

"When do you want me to go down there?"

"Imah have my lawyer come down there tomorrow and get it with you. Make sure you have him sign something, Granny."

"I will baby. What they talking bout? What they gonna do with y'all?"

"Well we might be going to the military if things work out. I love you, Granny."

"I love you too, Rudy."

★★★★★

Granny knew what it was. She knew the police in the south was dirty and could be brought. She just leaned back and close her eyes.

"Granny, what did he say?"

"Well, they got the lawyer and he said they might could buy their way outta these mess. The lawyer will be here tomorrow."

"Well that's some good news, huh?"

"Yes lord it is."

★★★★★

Two days later standing in front of a judge not saying anything Rudy and Zack were giving suspended sentences providing they go to the military.

Sitting in the back of the courtroom was Sergeant Smith and his cousins observing everything.

"We gonna stay on that old black bitch. She gots our fucking the money, I bet'cha."

"We should fucking kidnap her nigger azz right when she leaves and make her take us to the fucking money and the reefers."

"I'm willing to bet your ass boy it ain't round here. Probably in the bank getting washed through they fucking store they got."

"You don't say? So what we gonna do now, huh?"

"Boy, look here. I'm the law. I'm gonna bust they fucking azz sho as hell come."

"On what danggon charges?"

"Hold your horses, you just let me figure that out boy. 'Til I do, I'm keep a close tab on their black azz everywhere they go."

They mean mugged the boys unnoticed as they walked out the courtroom. Later that evening, they left from the police station straight to the recruiting office. The next morning they were both sitting on a bus headed for boot camp. In the back of the courtroom sat Sergeant Smith fuming at the mouth. He couldn't believe it. This shit ain't over, he thought. Fuck that. I'm get those fuckers one way or another.

★★★★★

Back in Greensboro in a courtroom sat Rico looking over at lil Johnny who was on the stand telling everything. When lil Johnny got off the stand Rico lawyer, who was the same lawyer Zack and Rudy had, walked over to the D.A.

"Can we strike a deal?"

"What kinda deal you talking bout Rilestien?"

"Listen instead of you trying to get the death sentence, which you know you won't get on him in this state, even with a cop killing, he will plead guilty to murder and 15 to 20 years."

"15 to 20 years for murdering a police officer, are you crazy?"

"It was a shootout not like he hunted him down."

The D.A. sat back and thought for a moment then nodded his head in agreement.

"Okay let me talk to the judge."

Within minutes, Rico was walking out of the courtroom back in to the holding cell. Now with 15 to 20 years to serve, all he could think of was who he could get to go get his money he had buried. He knew he couldn't tell no one but Rudy but how was he gonna get in touch with Rudy? He had to contact Granny soon before someone went to his house. Damn this shit went bad fast, he thought.

★★★★★

Sitting on the bus looking out the window was Rudy. He looked over at his childhood friend Zack.

He was the closest he had to a brother.

"Well Rudy you finally gonna get that uniform you always wanted."

"Yeah it looks like it huh?"

They both started laughing.

"Rudy, you think it's cool if my moms comes and picks up my part of the money from the store every week from Granny?"

"Yeah that's cool. If she wants she can go and work there with her on the weekend."

"She's keeping an eye on my Dad, trying hard to keep him straight."

"You got your money buried good, don't you?"

"Yeah a hound would never find it."

"Cool cause when we get outta here, we moving our families to California. I done had enough of the south. You wit me, Zack?"

"You know I'm with you all the way buddy, fo' life."

Rudy leaned back in the seat and thought he knew what he had to do get in here. Play their game. He knew deep in his heart he was far from ending his hustling career. This was only a pause in the play, to re−evaluate things. They had enough money stashed. I'm far from finished, he thought. This time it's gonna be me and Zack. That's it. No one to tell on me. Fuck the Air force and they uniform. I'm learn how to fly them planes so I can fill them with reefer and fly it home.

"Listen, soon as we get there, call your uncle in California. Let him know Granny, Ms. Irene and your folks moving out there. So ask him if he can start looking for a place for them both, okay?"

"I got you, Rudy. I got you."

They both closed their eyes and fell into a sleep until they heard, "Okay you soldiers, it's time to learn to fight. Get up and out. Now. Move it! Move it! Move it!" They were at the boot camp. Through Rudy dazed eyes he saw the barracks that occupied the dusty grounds. He looked over at Zack who was staring out the window.

"We had no choice, Rudy."

"Don't worry buddy. We gonna make the best of this, Zack. Yes, we is."

CHAPTER 5

It was awhile before Rudy realized that they hadn't even left North Carolina. Yet, he was deep in the mountains somewhere at a boot camp called Fort Jackson, a place surrounded by hills and made up of obstacles courses, shooting ranges, climbing maneuvers and a land field to teach them how to spot explosives and a long landing strip for the planes. Their daily routine was getting up at 4am running 5 miles during exercise, having breakfast, then coming back to the barracks to get ready for more training. It was school till noon. They always went to flight school at noon, learning how to fly the jets. This was Rudy's favorite. He love learning to fly. He had it down pat within three months. Zack took a little longer to catch on but he was getting there. Time flew fast before they knew it they were standing at graduation, finally being accepted into the United States Air Force.

That night, Rudy called Granny. Not having heard her voice in a few months it was a warming sound to his ears. Zack was on the other phone talking to his moms who was so proud of him and his father was doing real good completely sober for the last six months. Zack couldn't believe it.

"So how is everything going with the store Granny?"

"I haven't had no problems. Everything is going good."

"Does Zack moms come and get his share weekly?"

"Yes she does and even helps out on the weekends. And that dad of his is hard to get rid of."

"What you mean Granny?"

"Well since he stopped drinking, he wanna fix everything. Sometimes he fixes the same thang twice. Drives me crazy."

"Well I guess it's better than him being drunk."

"We so proud of y'all boys, we are."

"Granny, have you heard from Rico yet?"

"He hasn't written his momma yet but we got the address where he is. I guess he's still mad at the world."

"Yeah can you give me the address? I wanna make sure he knows I didn't just leave him."

"Listen, if you want I can send him a little something every month outta your money so he will be okay."

"That's cool, Granny, that's cool. I would like that." Rudy knew Rico had money stashed but probably hadn't figured out how to get to it yet. He didn't mind helping out his, Cuzn.

"Granny, I gotta go. I love you. I will call you when we get to where they sending us, okay?"

"Boy, you be careful and don't try to be no hero. You heard me?"

"Yes, ma'am. Love you, Granny."

"Love you too, Rudy."

★★★★★

Their first job was tour duty in Bangkok, Thailand.

"Damn this shit happens fast," said Zack.

"Yeah just think we was living the country boy hunter life not even 6 months ago now here we are bout to play G.I. Joe."

"Well I'm not gonna be no handicap hero for them Rudy. We got 4 years and we out this bitch."

"You damn right, homey. You damn right."

After the ceremony, the fellows went to sleep. The next morning they were on a flight headed for Thailand. A long flight, with their uniforms, on gear packed up and ready for whatever. Rudy and Zack sat on the plane flying high in the sky over the ocean headed for Thailand.

They landed and got settled in. It was like they were in the middle of the jungle somewhere. Brush and tall trees, weird noises at night filled the air. It was a long landing strip located in the middle of the grounds. Every morning a platoon would go up in the air practicing shooting and destination maneuvers.

After sixty days Rudy and Zack were ready for combat.

"So you ready to go kill the enemy?"

"Ready as I'll ever be, buddy."

"It's the same thang as we did when we were boys, except now we got people shooting back at us."

"Yeah that's a big difference."

"Don't worry. Granny praying for us."

Within minutes it seemed like the boys were in the air flying. Through the air outta nowhere, Rudy saw an enemy plane coming toward him. He didn't panic. He focused in and squeezed the trigger slowly and shot it down. Then they kept coming, one after another. Rudy gunned them down then they stopped coming. Rudy circled the surroundings and saw an enemy camp hidden deep in the woods. Gun blast emerged immediately. Rudy swooped down fast and let loose round after round at the camp, letting a bomb drop from his jet at the same time. A loud explosion followed with dust and body parts flying throughout the air. Rudy circled the grounds again. There was no movement. He radio in. He was told to fly back to the base. He had done an excellent job. Next day was the same thing. This continued for two weeks. Rudy and Zack attacking enemies in the air and on the ground. Before they knew it, they were the talk of the base — the two hot shot pilots, country boys from the south, were putting in major work for the Air Force.

Rudy and Zack got called in to the Colonel's office. He sat behind a big large wooden desk with pictures of former and current Air Force hero's all on his wall. He was a slim man with an extremely large head who chained smoked cigarettes one after another.

"Sit down, boys."

"Thank you, sir."

'Thank you."

"Well, I just wanted say you and your friend here are helping us win this war. Damn, you boys are amazing. How you learned to fly and shoot that good so damn fast?"

"Well, sir, we country boys. It comes natural shooting at things," Zack said smiling.

"Yes, sir, it's something we love to do."

"Well I must say I'm glad you on our side and we do like to reward our soldiers for their hard work. We have a special ceremony set up tonight. It's mandatory that you both attend."

"Thank you, sir. We will be there."

Both the boys walked out the office. Grinning from ear to ear on their way to the barracks to get their uniforms ironed up for tonight. After they finished they walked to the chow halls, bumping their gums. The word around the barracks was they were bout to get medals for their bravery in combat.

"This might not be too bad after all," said Zack.

"I don't like this place. Nothing bout it," said Rudy thinking about the racist system that he was really fighting for.

"What about that?"

"What?"

"Excuse me, big superstar. You gonna knock a little lady down like you been doing those camps and planes, huh?" said a pretty tan brown southern accented woman standing in front of Rudy, smiling.

"No, I didn't even see you. I'm sorry. Are you okay?"

"Yes, I am. So you the one I been hearing about, huh? The superstar pilot."

"I wouldn't say all that. I would say I'm blessed to be alive."

"Well that's a humble approach to warfare."

"My name is Rudy. And yours?"

"Maryann. Maryann Summers."

"Well it's a pleasure to make your acquaintance."

"Likewise, solider. I will see you at the ceremonies tonight maybe."

"Maybe." Maryann walked away.

Since Rudy had been there he really hadn't taken out time to converse with any woman. His mind was on his mission, learn to survive and get the hell outta that place. But this woman caught his attention plus he could tell from her accent she was from the country.

"Well big man I think you have your first female fan," Zack said laughing hitting Rudy on his shoulder.

"Have you ever seen her before? Damn she's pretty."

"That's the first time. I think she likes you though."

"Why would you say that?"

"She looked like she wanted to have you for dinner."

They both laughed and went into the chow hall. Since they were young boys girls really never got much attention from them. They had a few girlfriends but nothing too serious.

After chow, they went back to the barracks, got dressed and headed to the ceremony. It was an old warehouse turned in a plush hall with a home built stage. As the speaker for the night went through his routine, Rudy and Zack waited patiently. Then their names where called and they were given medals. As Rudy walked off to applause, he noticed Maryann standing up smiling and clapping looking him dead in the eye. He passed by her on his way back to his seat and winked at her. She smiled back and winked.

★★★★★

For the next three weeks when they could they spent as much time together as possible. Maryann was from Memphis, Tennessee, the rough part of town. She was the oldest of eleven children, so she felt it was her duty to get out the house and make room for more people at the dinner table. Her parents were still together proud of her. Her mother was a seamstress and her father worked at the local mill. Maryann had plans to go to college after the military. She really made her parents proud.

★★★★★

"Damn, Rudy. When we gonna go to town and kick it? You always under Maryann. You done forgot bout your boy."

"Not at all. I tell you what. She has duty this weekend, so let's go to town and hangout a little."

"Sounds good to me."

★★★★★

The week passed and there they were riding on a bus into Bangkok headed to a local pub that was a known hangout for soldiers.

As they walked in the dark lit place with red lights and loud American music playing with a long bar and some stairs that lead to the best sex a solider could afford. It didn't tale long to understand why it was the talk of the base. There were beautiful Thai women everywhere with little to nothing on.

"Damn I think Imah like this place," said Zack. Before he could get the words outta his mouth there were two cute girls all on his arms pulling him in the back of the club up towards those stairs.

"Zack, be careful keep your eyes open."

"I got this here, buddy, I got this."

Rudy sat back at the bar relaxing sipping on a beer. He didn't really drink that much, he was just taking in the atmosphere. A Thailand man talking to a white solider sat next to them. Rudy over heard the conversation the white solider owed the Thai man money for drugs. As Rudy looked closer, he could tell the solider was not in good health. He suspected drug use. He had never really seen dope fiends but he had heard how alotta soldiers over there were sprung on opium, pure heroin. The Thai man pulled a pistol from his waistline and put it to the soldiers stomach.

The solider looked at Rudy.

"Please, please, help me. This dude is crazy. I don't owe him nothing."

Rudy looked at the Thai man. "How much he owe you?"

"Four hundred American. Four hundred American or I kill him now right here."

Rudy was amazed how good of English the Thai man spoke. Rudy dug into his pocket and pulled out four one hundred dollar bills and handed them to the Thai man.

"Here you go. Is that all he owes you?"

"He no come here no more or he die. He die."

The white solider ran out the bar never even thanking Rudy. Zack was walking towards them now smiling. He had had a good time.

"What's going on?" Rudy explained to him what had just happened. "I hate to tell you buddy but I heard of that scam before. I think you just got played."

Right when Zack was saying that, Rudy noticed the Thai man sliding out his chair headed for the door.

"Let's go," said Rudy. They both followed the Thai man down the street to an alley and there he was – the solider standing there smiling. The Thai man handed the solider the money and he split it as Rudy and Zack watched him.

"Well I'll be damn ain't that something."

"So you gonna let them just take your money?"

"Hell no." Rudy walked up and punched the

solider in the mouth and grabbed the Thai man by the throat choking him. The man was almost breathless.

"Whatever you want, I get it. Whatever you want, I get it," the Thai man said between gagging breaths. Rudy let loose of him for a moment as the white solider got up from the ground.

"Please don't kill us. You got your money back. I'm strung out, man. Please don't kill us. What do you want? Guns? Girls? Dope? Whatever you want I can get you."

Zack looked at Rudy.

"Are you on the base?"

"Yes. My name is Leroy Miles. I'm from Kentucky, just trying to get back home. I came over here and got this monkey on my back. Please don't kill me."

"I ain't gonna kill you. I'm gonna help you, if you help me."

"Whatever you want."

"Sit down, both you." The men leaned against the wall nervously. "So what's the rundown with this opium over here?"

"What do you mean?"

"How much does a pound cost in American money?"

"They don't sell pounds only kilos. If you want a large amount but I can get you something for one hundred dollars if you wanna try it."

"Hell no we don't wanna try it. For what to be like you?" Zack said.

"Well how much is a kilo in American money?" Rudy said.

"Ten thousand and you can make a quarter mill with the cut on it in the States easy."

Zack eyes lit up and so did Rudy's. "Is that

right?"

"I tell you what. Think of this as your lucky night. Imah let y'all live. I'll see you back at the base," Rudy said as he went through both their pockets retrieving his money.

The boys walked back out the alley. "So what you think? You think that's legit?"

"Well I'm definitely gonna check into ASAP."

"That's sound like alotta money to be made."

"You damn right it does. Listen when we get back, call your uncle and talk to him. You said he was a gangster, right?"

"You damn right he is."

"Well ask him does those prices sound right and does he thinks it safe to send that shit over there."

"I'm on it." The boys got on the bus and headed for the barracks in silence. Rudy sat there was thinking about his cousin Rico and that twenty years in prison that he was doing, about the racist security guard in the store and what he had did to Granny. He had a year and a half left to give these people. He knew that and he knew when he got back in the real world it would take money to live like he wanted to. He went out to meet Maryann at their usual spot there she was waiting on a blanket in the grass.

"Hey baby, how you doing?"

"I'm okay," she said smiling up at him.

"What's wrong with you?"

"Nothing, really, just thinking about when I get outta this military, what I really wanna do," he said sitting down and kissing her.

"So what is that may I ask?"

"I wanna move my Granny to California and

make a good life for her."

"What about your life Rudy?"

"I wanna get married and have me some kids and live like I deserve to."

"And how is that?"

"With no worries,"

"And you will. You a strong man, powerful and smart and brave. I really like you, Rudy."

They both leaned in and kissed each other passionately Maryann had never been with a man before. Rudy was her first and she was his as they laid on the blanket in the grass holding each other in their arms it seemed like time had stopped.

"Well, it's getting late baby. We better go."

"Time sure goes fast when you having fun."

"Yes it does."

"I need to tell you something, Rudy."

"What's that?"

"My Captain said I will be getting transferred to Texas next week. Back to the States."

"Why did you wait so long to tell me?"

"I just found out today. I was going to tell you when we sat down but it seemed like you had too much on your mind."

"So what's gonna happen with us?"

"To be honest with you, you're the first man I ever liked besides my Daddy. I don't know what to think. When I think of you sometimes it scares me."

"Why is that?"

"Because I think I'm falling in love with you, that's why." Maryann got up and ran to her barracks, leaving Rudy sitting there with his mouth open.

★★★★★

The days passed fast. Zack had spoken to his

uncle once he had told him to call back. He had some underworld former military buddies he had to check with first. They knew more about the current streets. When Zack called back, he told him it was all good. They could benefit and his friends could move it for him, it was a go. Rudy had Granny transfer forty thousand in his account. She got twenty thousand from Zack's mother. Now it was about preparing for the buy. The question was how was he gonna get it to California?

Sitting on his bunk in the barracks, Rudy brain stormed. He looked up and noticed a solider putting a box together to send home. He went over and started a conversation with him picking his brain about how the shipping works. From what he got, all Rudy had to do was stuff products full of opium and it would be sent to the address with no problem. Now he began to think, a few kilos ain't enough. I gotta get more to make it worth my while but how can I do that.

In walks the white solider who had try to scam him outta his money.

"Hey there buddy how you doing?"

"I'm okay. What about yourself?"

"I been staying clean. I got like three months left and I'm home. I really thank you for letting us go that night. I was doing some stupid stuff messing around with these drugs."

"Yeah that could have got you killed my friend. So what you plan on doing when you get outta here?"

"My family owns a garage so I'm go work in there until I can get a government job."

"Listen if you can be trusted I got a situation for you that you will be able to make alotta money fast if you can keep your mouth closed."

"Is that right? By doing what?"

"First do you think you can trust that Thai man at all?"

"I been over here three years, he's all I been dealing with and I know he has the connects to everything in Thailand."

"Yeah but what makes you think you can trust him?"

"He thinks he going home with me."

"And how you gonna arrange that?"

"I'm not. That was to keep him at bay."

Rudy thought for a minute. I can't trust this dude but I gotta get that connect.

"Listen tell him we wanna meet the head man. We gonna spend forty thousand American money. I don't wanna talk to no one else. Can you arrange that?"

"I'm pretty sure I can. Let me contact you after work and I'll get back in touch with you."

"What's up?" said Zack walking over to Rudy's bunk coming from outside.

"I just hollered at that solider. He's gonna go holler at the Thai man."

"Rudy, we got a lot to lose buddy."

"I know. I want you to go to intelligence and holler at that blonde always smiling at you and find out everything we can bout that solider just in case."

"I'm on it." Zack hurried out the barracks headed for the blonde.

That night the solider came back and told Rudy he had the meeting set up.

The next evening Zack and Rudy headed into town with the solider. They went to a small restaurant on the main strip. It was multi colored with Thailand symbols painted all on the walls. Red carpet lined the walls and pretty waitress catered to the patrons. There sat the Thai man with two other Thai men. Both had on sunglasses. Zack and Rudy and the solider walked to the table and sat down.

"So what's up? Do y'all speak English?"

"Yes they do. What is it you want?"

"First, I don't wanna talk to you. I wanna talk to them. Listen I need your product and I don't need no bullshit. I spend alotta American money with you if it ain't no problems can you handle that."

"How much you wanna spend?" said one of the Thai men.

"I have forty thousand American dollars to spend with you. I need five of those pies for that."

"So you want one for free?"

"Not for free. For me coming back with more money each time," Rudy said.

"You a funny man. Very funny man," said the other one then. They begin speaking in Thai language. Rudy stood up nodding at Zack to leave.

"Hold on solider, hold on," one of the Thai men said.

"What's up?" Rudy said.

"Have a sit. We can talk. We can talk."

They sat there with the Thai men for maybe twenty minutes and workout out the details. They were in business. They would meet tomorrow the shook hands and left.

"Listen we gonna meet you back at the barracks," Rudy told the white solider.

"Why what's up?"

"Oh we have a few other things to do."

"Okay, I'll see you when you get back." The solider walked off.

"Did you get the background check on that dude?"

"I got everything. His Granddaddy social security if we need it."

"Good we might be needing it. Tonight get his home number also his whole families numbers."

Zack looked at Rudy strangely he knew Rudy was plotting on something. They went into an oil and incense store.

"Yes, yes. Do you have the peppermint oil?" asked Rudy. It was what Maryann use. Rudy had found out from the solider you could also use this oil to test the potency of the opium. He was also gonna use some meat fats from the kitchen to decoy the drug smell if the dogs got on the package. Zack just stood back and watch. Rudy paid for the oil and they walked back to the bus stop and got on the bus.

"We gonna be okay, buddy," Rudy ensured Zack.

"I'm wit you all the way."

"I know that, Zack. I know that."

Finally arriving at the base they went to the canteen. Rudy brought a big stereo system and they walked back to the barracks and prepared for bed.

The next evening they were at the same restaurant waiting on the Thai men to show up. Zack was getting antsy keeping his hand on his gun the whole time. Rudy was calm thinking to himself, ten of these moves and we gonna stack enough kilos so when we come home we won't ever have to go to no one in the states for nothing and never run out until we super rich. The white solider was sitting at the table next to Rudy and Zack looking nervous.

"You okay buddy?"

"Yeah I'm okay," he said drinking his water shaking. Rudy had him there to carry the package back to the base. In walked the two Thai men. They came over and sat down carry a duffle bag.

"So what's up?" Rudy said. They slide the bag beside Rudy and opened it Rudy took a kilo and put it in his lap and pull out a knife cut into it. He drop a little of the powder into a testing bottle he had put together that night. He waited and it came back damn near pure. Rudy looked at the Thai men and smiled. Then tested the other four kilos. They were all good. He looked at Zack and nodded his head. Zack passed the Thai men their money.

"Don't worry, we own the place and the town. See you we you ready again."

"Most definitely." Zack got up and so did Rudy grabbing the duffle bag on his way out he handed it to the white solider.

"Meet me back at the barracks."

"I got you."

"Ay, I spoke to your grandpa the other night in Kentucky. Your dog Waggle is doing okay. Let's makes sure things stay that way."

"What?" The white solider looked at Zack amazed and shunned. He knew what he was saying. "Don't fuck up or get smart with our shit." He continued to walk out the door.

"Make sure you go straight to the barracks buddy."

"I will. Don't worry."

Rudy and Zack watch as the solider got on the bus and headed for the barracks They walked around the corner and got into a jeep they had borrowed from base They did so they would be with the solider and also to beat him to the base and they had paid the bus driver to radio them immediately if the white solider did anything funny. Standing in the barracks window was Rudy and Zack waiting on the bus to arrive. There it was and off walked the white solider. He came right into the barracks and handed Rudy the duffle bag. Rudy opened it up and handed it to Zack. Zack disappeared. He went in the back and began stuffing the product into the speakers of the stereo system Rudy had brought then he boxed it up and took it to the mailroom the whole time. Rudy kept the white solider with him till Zack came back. Finally in walks Zack.

"We good, Rudy." Within days the package was at Zack's Uncle Pete's spot and it didn't take him and his Buddies no time to get it off. They gave Granny (who was out there in California as Rudy had planned at the same time house hunting with Ms. Irene and Unc Pete) 300,000 thousand, a 150,000 apiece for Rudy and Zack and they kept 100,000 to split three ways. Everyone was happy.

"That wasn't that bad at all."

"Hell nall. You ready? Let's go meet our boys." The boys were walking towards the jeep to do their second run, never seeing Maryann walking up behind them holding her bags.

"Hey stranger." Rudy reached for his gun, startled Maryann, stopped in her tracks, dropping her bags.

"Dang don't shoot me."

"I'm sorry."

"So you just wanna disappear since I told you I was transferring huh?" It had totally slipped Rudy's mind his girl was leaving. Damn he had been so busy it slipped his mind.

"No it ain't like that I been on extra duty."

"Extra duty, yeah right. I seen you moving around here like a cat a few times."

"Listen you know how I feel. It wasn't easy for me when you told me that."

"So what are you gonna stay in touch with me?"

Rudy noticed the bags finally looking down in her hand. Damn she was bout to leave, he realized.

"I promise. I will. I'm come find you." Rudy handed Zack the duffle bag of money and walked over and hugged and kissed Maryann.

"I care a lot bout you. Never forget that."

"Just don't stop writing me. I'm write you as soon as I get there in Texas. Bye baby. I love you." She kissed him and walked away. Rudy stood there for a moment then got into the jeep.

"You okay buddy?"

"Yeah I'm cool. Let's go. Is the solider in town waiting?"

"Yeah he should be or definitely bout to get there. I sent him like a hour ago."

For the next year Rudy and Zack did monthly runs sending their product and getting paper. Granny stacked their Money for them, never asking any questions. Everything was going smooth. Time had went so fast Rudy didn't realize he was six months to the house.

"Rudy what's up buddy?" Zack said walking up to Rudy who was relaxing in the grass thinking bout life reading a letter from Maryann.

"I just got word. Rudy we're going to California Travis base in two days. We finally going home."

"Now how you know all that?"

"The blonde, my man, the blonde."

Rudy started smiling from ear to ear. Damn it would be good to be back in the USA. They had money stacked and alotta dope waiting on them. All he had to do now was knock out these last six months and where better to do it at than at home soil. Rudy stood up and hugged his buddy. This was one of the happiest days of his life. They walked back into the barracks and began packing their things. That night they went into town and met the Thai man for the last time. Two days later they were in the blue skies headed for the good old USA.

"Damn this feels good, Rudy."

"It's bout to get a lot better, Zack. It's bout to get a lot better." Rudy said as the plane pierced through the clouds and sky.

CHAPTER 6

It was a hot scorching day the sun rays could be seen coming off the road as the tumble weeds blows down the field. It was a clear sky and you could see for miles. This was Texas, east Texas near Houston. The base was fairly small used for special missions and services it was no more than twenty barracks there and a few other tin building lining the dirt cover ground with a large landing strip and building to store the airplanes in. It had barely no grass in sight it was extremely humid during this time of year luckily for Maryann her most physical training outdoors was over with she was a weapons expert who handle the logging in and out of the missiles that were placed on the jets so basically she sat in a cool office all day and filed paperwork and thought of Rudy, the love of her life, at lunch often since she had been there she would pull out his old letters or go to the mail call hoping to receive one this was her first love and the only one she wanted,

Coming to the end of one of Rudy letter it read.

"my love, my every day is filled with thoughts of our past visions of our future and anticipation of the moments we see each other again. those were the happiest times of my life in your arms. I know we have more waiting on us.

I love you. yours truly, Rudy"

★★★★★

Back in Buford, South Carolina at the local police station not even two months later stands a former security guard but now known as Sergeant Smith, standing there all proud he was being inducted into the chief of police position. He even hired his two cousins later that week as deputies.

"Well cousin, we got the power now. All we got to do is sit back and wait and watch."

"Fuck, yeah. This is easiest fucking shit I ever did."

"Hell yeah. We bust fuckers coming in with dope and take it and their money and it's legal. We should've been doing this shit."

"Well just don't forget the main reason you deputies is to bust open that fucking niggers operation. I know they still up to something. That black old bitch be driving round here like she the fucking mayor or something. I want twenty four hour surveillance put on her at all times. Put the word out. I'm get his azz, Air Force hero or not, soon as he gets his azz back in this town. And I got a buddy in the FBI, good ole boy white breaded, you know he gonna be on their azz as well."

"I'll pass the word on to the deputies' chief."

"Thanks. Do it right away."

"Well let me go get me some niggers right now and lock they asses up. Put them monkeys in cages like they belong."

"I bet'cha I get twenty tonight."

"Shit I'm get twenty five."

"Bet a weeks pay. Bet a weeks pay." They laughed walking out the door to their patrol cars like cowboys with Chief Smith standing in his office door smiling like a proud poppa.

*****

Across town Granny was sitting in her large living room staring at her wooden shellacked floors, the long velvet curtains hanging open over the windows. Most of her big beautiful pictures of black soldiers had already been taken down. She hadn't had this house that long but she had feel in love with it. She would still own it and rent it out but Rudy said it was best for her to move to California and get from down in the racist south. He told her she could bring Ms. Irene and her husband with her. He would buy them a house also right next to hers so she couldn't refuse even though this was her home. She always wanted to leave since she was a little girl. Sitting there watching the moving men carry her belongings out the door was bitter sweet as a few tears ran down her face.

"Granny. Granny."

"Huh?" She turned around startled. It was Ms. Irene.

"We got everything in the trucks. Dang I didn't know I had that much stuff."

"Where is Harold?" That was Ms. Irene husband. A quiet man, painter by trade, he was a homebody and one woman man. Small in build with African features large lips and very dark. A good church going man, Ms. Irene was very happily married. She had to talk him into moving to California but he was tired of the south also.

"He's sitting on the porch sipping on some of your famous lemonade."

"Gal, I'm gonna miss this place."

"Yeah I know you will, but you will fall in love with California in no time."

"I sho will be glad when Rudy come on home."

"Them boys ain't got that much longer and they done did good for themselves in there getting all them medals and stuff."

"Yeah I'm proud of them."

"Granny let me ask you something. Did you call the police or sheriff?"

"No. Why you ask that?"

"Well the police car been sitting cross the street not moving for the last two hours since the trucks got here."

"Is that right? You know I think they been following me lately. I know I ain't crazy, I know they is now."

"I wonder what's that all about?"

"Jealously. They hate to see black folks not struggling. That's all it is."

"Well they ain't gotta worry bout us no more. We outta here."

They both laughed and hugged as Granny got up and looked one last time at her old southern big house Rudy had brought her.

"Well we leaving. Y'all can handle the rest of the stuff right, sir?" Granny said to a black gentlemen who was working for someone Rudy had sent down there to move their stuff cross country.

"Yes, ma'am. We got everything but the curtains. That's next."

"Okay well we going to the hotel. We leaving in the morning, first flight. We'll see you in California."

"Good night, ma'am. Have a good flight. See you in California."

Granny, Ms. Irene, and Harold jumped in Ms. Irene's car and headed for the hotel to go to sleep and get ready to leave the south in the morning.

"These fuckers are moving again."

"Say what?"

"Hell yeah they been hauling shit out that big house all day."

"What moving company moving them?"

"I ain't ever seen them before. I think they from outta town."

"Is that right? Well what's going on now?"

"Them old ladies just left it looks like they bout finished packing and ready to leave."

"When the ladies leave find out where them movers from and where they taking that shit to immediately."

"Okay I got you, Chief."

"Get off the fucking phone and do your job then." He hung up angry.

"Damn, he's mad."

"Shit it was our money and reefer them fuckers stole to get all this. Do you remember dumb azz?"

"Fuck you. Let's find out where this shit going." The deputy said as he got out the passenger side of the car and went walking towards the front door. When they both got there the door was cracked so they went on in.

"Hey there how you doing boss?"

Startled one of the movers turned around. "What's going on officer? What's the problem?"

"Well, we just passing through. Been having alotta break−ins in this area. We just making sure everything is alright. So where y'all moving all this stuff to? They selling this house?"

"I don't know. We driving it to California, outside of Oakland was the orders. That's all I know."

"Is that right? California huh? Outside of Oakland? Well I'll be damn that's a good place to move. Y'all boys take it easy." The deputies walked out the door straight to their car. They called their chief immediately.

"Chief, they moving to California. Them fuckers are rich off our shit. I should go kill that black old bitch right now, Chief."

"Calm your azz down and meet me back at the station. I got a phone call to make."

The chief hung up and dialed his buddy in the FBI and explained to him that he had some major drug dealers under surveillance and he needed some help finding out what they were up to nationwide. The FBI man told him it would be no problem. He would contact the California Oakland office immediately and have someone waiting to keep surveillance on this family.

CHAPTER 7

It was a breezy foggy morning sun shining through the hills and green forest land of Thailand through the window of the barracks. The sun rays bounced off Rudy's forehead. Zack was already up and ready. Finally. He couldn't believe it. They were leaving Thailand and headed back to America.

"Wake up sleepy head. It's time to go, boss. We going home, buddy."

"That was fast. It felt like I just was sitting here talking to you last night," Rudy said getting up outta bed.

"Well listen go ahead and get ready. I'm go call Uncle Pete, check on Granny and moms while you getting ready."

"Sounds like a plan, my friend. I'll be ready in about twenty minutes." Rudy stopped for a minute and looked around the barracks it had been almost a year and a half he had been there he hadn't seen his beloved Grandma. Damn it would be good to get outta here. Then he thought about what this place had brought him — pilot skills in air and on the ground, the love of his life Maryann, and the product that would fund him the rest of his life. He began smiling as he gathered his belongs and placed them at the door waiting for his friend Zack to return.

"Well everything is okay in California. Word from Uncle Pete but moms says the police been following her she thinks."

"Say what?"

"Yeah my moms said she thinks the police been following her and Granny said that racist police is behind it, the same one that was the security guard when you were little. She said you knew who she was talking bout. Well he is the police chief in Buford now."

"Well I'll be damned. Ain't that something?"

"When we get to California, first thing we do before we make any moves, is look into what that crooked cop is up to."

"Rudy, I'm just glad we getting our folks outta there."

"Yeah it sounds like in the nick of time, buddy."

"You think they know bout the reefer we took?"

"They got to but so what? We good American hero's now headed home with legit businesses. They can't do nothing."

"Yeah we need to get our store the hell from down there immediately also when we get back."

"You right bout that, Zack. You right about that."

"Well let's go. There's our ride." The boys said their good byes to the soldiers in the barracks and got into the jeep and were driven to the air strip. Within minutes they were in the air flying through the skies piercing the clouds of the international upper roads. Both slept most of the time headed for America. It took little over twelve hours but finally they were preparing for landing at the Travis Air Force base. Rudy and Zack waking up between times then going back to sleep.

"Say buddy you woke? We here, we here!" Rudy said.

"Huh?"

"We here. We here we in California. Wake up, wake up."

The announcement came over the intercom to buckle up prepare for landing then they descended to the ground bumping and braking and finally coming to a stop. They looked at each other and smiled then they peeped out the window at the base. It was a large facility with the entrance lined with palm trees along the manicured lawn. Old former jet planes sat in the yard sitting up proudly for view. Upon entering the grounds there was a large building with soldiers coming in and out. They knew that was the PX were they would do most of their shopping on base, later on after getting settled in and reporting to all the units they were supposed to.

They still had a whole day to waste because they didn't have to be back for duty until the next morning so they decided to get a jeep and drive down to Oakland and visit Unc Pete and Granny to check on everything and see how they were doing. Riding down the highways of California was wonderful with the large mountains and ocean staring at them as they passed by it. It was almost 200 miles to Oakland, and the boys blasted the latest on the music on the radio laughing all the way.

"There it is. San Leandro city limits. Take this exit," said Rudy.

San Leandro was a large Mexican community, the suburb right outside Oakland that Unc Pete stayed in and where Granny had moved to. It had modern houses on the flatlands instead of the hills like in Oakland. It was mostly a working class community.

"It looks like it's pretty safe round here."

"Yeah Unc Pete been living here all his life. He says the danger is up the streets of Oakland."

"And the money too from what I've heard, Zack."

"Ain't this the street we looking for right here?"

"Martin Avenue. Yeah. Turn here. We looking for 1225 Martin Avenue." They drove down a ways.

"There it is right there." The boys pulled in the drive way and blew the horn. Out walking slowly was an elderly white man with a grey beard and bald head using a cane with a slight limp.

"Well, I'll be damn. Boy, you done grew into a man," Unc Pete said to Zack as he got out the car.

"And it look like you ain't aged a bit since I was a little boy." Unc Pete been gray since he was in his thirties.

"And this must be, Rudy," he said extending his hand.

"You my Uncle now. You gotta give me a hug." Rudy leaned in and hugged Unc Pete. They both laughed.

"Thank you for being straight with us," Rudy whisper in his ear.

"Listen I'm a solider that loves my country but I love my family first. I was told how you been like brothers your whole life. I would never cross you. Now, let's go inside so we can talk."

They walked in the house and sat down in the sparely furnished house. It had an American flag on the wall and all kinds of medals Unc Pete had won during the war and large picture of him in his uniform.

"Wow. This you Unc Pete?" Rudy said looking at the photo.

"Yeah that's was in my fighting days. I could knock down forty planes a day."

"Damn for real?"

"Well from what I understand y'all two ain't no joke either."

"We ain't nothing compared to this."

"Always remember, son, times cause different kinds of war. The key to war is deception. Always remember that and you will win. This war on the street is no different." They all sat down on the couch.

"So did everything go good on the last run?"

"Everything is fine and waiting on y'all. We all stacked up."

"Okay cool."

"So let us get settled in then we gonna make a move this weekend. Knock the rest of these down little by little and invest the proceeds."

"Now that's what I'm talking bout. Invest."

"What you got in mind, Unc Pete?"

"I was thinking a chain of garages, auto mechanic shops. It will always have business."

"Well, we gonna look into it, definitely."

"So, when the last time you talked to Granny?"

"Well I just got off the phone with her. I'm either on the phone with them or over there every day."

"How far do they live from here?"

"Oh I got them something close to me they right around the corner."

"Thank you. Thank you for looking out for Granny like that."

"Hell it was nothing. That lady there has alotta spunk. She is alright with me, yes she is. I would do anything for her."

"Yeah she's hard not to love."

"Well let's go surprise them. They don't even know we here yet."

"Let's go then." They all got up. Unc Pete grabbed his coat. They walked out the door and hopped in the jeep and headed down the road.

"Turn right here, nephew."

"Okay got'cha."

"Go down to the next street and turn left. It's the big green house with the yellow trimming."

"Where does Ms. Irene live at?"

"Right next door in the brown house."

"Ay that's alright. I like that. Thanks again, Unc Pete."

They pulled in the driveway, its entrance to a beautiful stucco home, large windows, white yellow shutters to match the trimming. The shrubbery in the front was cut perfect like it had its own barber and the small front lawn was short green and no dirt. Rudy couldn't see it but the back was Granny's hang out, the garden that she turned into South Carolina in California. The boys and Unc Pete walked up to the door and ranged the doorbell.

It took a minute but Granny open the door smiling with what looked like tears in her eyes. She was wearing a terrycloth pretty pink robe.

"Lord knows you a sight for sore eyes. Come mere, baby." She walked into Rudy's arms.

"Hey Granny, how you doing? I missed you so much. I missed you so much." Tears came outta Rudy eyes. It had been two and a half years since he had seen Granny. They loved each other unconditionally.

"Let me look at you boy. My goodness what they been feeding you? And look at you, Zack. Come mere, son."

Zack almost leaped into Granny arms hugging her. Having been sitting back in awe witnessing the love Granny and Rudy shared. Zack parents was on the way next month. Zack's mom had to finish wrapping things up at the store since they were about to transfer the business to California.

"Hey there Granny. How you doing?" Zack said smiling.

"I'm okay, for an old lady."

"It looks like you getting younger to me," Rudy said putting his hand on Granny's shoulder.

"Well I can't get no hug? Dang."

Rudy and Zack turned around they knew the voice they had heard it their whole life. It was Ms. Irene.

"Of course you can. How you doing, Ms. Irene?"

"Hey there, Rudy. You done got big boy. All grown up now. And Zack was you picking up planes or flying them?"

Zack had gotten extremely muscular doing his training looking something like a body builder.

"Well sit down, rest your feet."

"Unc Pete, you want something?"

"Yes, please. Let me get a beer."

Rudy and Zack looked at each other. They never knew Granny to keep liquor in her house.

"Irene, can you bring this rascal a beer?" Unc Pete came by so much it was like he lived there. He brought his own case of beer and kept it cold in the fridge. Granny didn't mind. He told good old war stories at night in the back yard.

"Baby, how long can y'all stay?"

"Well, we just got in today."

"Yup, just landed and got checked in and came straight to see you."

"No y'all didn't. Y'all went to Pete's house first," Granny said.

"Well, we didn't know where you lived, that's why, Granny," Zack said. They all started laughing.

"Well, what time y'all gotta be back?"

"We gotta be back for duty by in the morning."

"Well, we got enough time to have a good dinner and talk."

"Let me go in the kitchen. Come on Irene." Granny got up and headed for the kitchen followed by Ms. Irene.

"Let me call over to the house and tell Harold I'm cooking over here tonight."

"How is Mr. Harold doing? Does he like California?"

"He's okay he complains about the high price of living out here and the violence and too many people all the time but he loves it. Always trying to run off somewhere with Pete." Ms. Irene said looking at Pete.

Unc Pete had a love for strip clubs which Harold loved to go to and Ms. Irene knew that. She really didn't want her husband going there wasting money but put up with it sometimes.

"Rudy, come through here and go out back and see the garden, baby. I got your favorites in there."

"Okay. Here we come."

"Y'all go ahead. I'm sit here for a minute. I'll back there," said Unc Pete as the boys walked into the kitchen headed for the back door.

"Rudy, come mere baby."

"Yes, ma'am."

Granny pulled Rudy close to her and looked him in the eyes. "Thank you so much for getting this house for me and getting me out that south."

"Yes, lord, thank you, Zack and Rudy." Ms. Irene said as she hung up the phone and came over to them all.

"Well, we owe you Granny. You helped us so much."

"Baby, I know you boys did some wrong. But no matter what, always remember, you my boys. Granny gonna always be here for you. You hear me?"

"Yes, ma'am," the boys said together and everyone started laughing again.

"I know y'all wanna talk bout y'all money. I ain't spent it. It's safe don't worry. We gonna talk. Let me finish this food."

The boys looked at each other and smiled. "We wasn't."

"I know you better than yourself. We gonna talk."

"Yeah, y'all get outta here."

"Zack, you stay in here and call your Momma first though, son."

"Yeah you right Granny. Thank you." Zack walked and grabbed the phone off the wall and dialed his moms home number. After a few rings he heard her voice.

"Hello."

"Hey there pretty lady. How you?"

Unc Pete walked by headed for the back yard to talk to Rudy. "Tell your momma I said hello, Zack."

"Zack! Hey son. Where you at?"

"I'm in California at Granny's house with Ms. Irene and Unc Pete. He said hello by the way."

"Yeah I heard his loud mouth. When did y'all get there?"

"We got to California early in the day and drove down here."

"Why you take so long to call me?"

"Momma I'm sorry we was rushing to get off the base and get here."

"You don't love your momma no more?"

"You know better than that don't even try it."

"So how long y'all there for?"

"We just eating dinner then going back to the base. We gotta report to duty in the morning. Were's dad at?"

"He went to a meeting. He's really been doing good, Zack."

"That's good, Momma, that's good. How's the store going?"

"It's going good. I'm almost got things ready. The inventory getting close so hopefully we can get out there next month."

"Good, cause I can't wait to see you."

"Listen, Zack, the sheriff been sitting outside the house and coming past the store a lot. I think they following me or something. Is everything alright son?"

"Yeah momma, don't worry. We'll take care of it."

"Son, I'm proud of you and thank you so much for the house and the business. It helps your father. I told you he would come around."

"Yeah you did, Mom. You did."

"We'll let me check on his food, son. I love you and I will see you soon."

"Okay Moms love you and tell dad I love him too."

"Tell everyone I said hello. Goodnight."

"Goodnight, Momma." Zack placed the phone on the wall handle and walked out the back door.

"Zack. Just the man we need to see. Sit down, son," said Unc Pete.

"So listen boys. Everything is ready like I said."

"Can you be more specific?" Rudy said as Zack edged up in his chair.

"Well, we started with four pies. We split that profit."

"Right. After that we said hold two every time till we get here."

"And that's what I did. We got 2.7 million dollars for you, which Granny has and 16 pies left."

"Say what?"

"Unc Pete, how much?"

"2.7 million dollars and 16 pies left for you."

"Motherfucking right shitted," Zack yelled.

"Now I'm need half a million from both of you for the houses we bought for your folks. I did that outta my money."

"No problem, Unc, no problem."

"Shit, we still sitting pretty."

"You fucking right. So listen, I need you boys to take it easy and don't do nothing stupid. Get out that Air Force so we can go to work and while you still in there stack us some artillery much as you can."

"I got you, Unc. I got you."

"So listen, we'll come back this weekend and take a ride okay?"

"Sound good to me. Only Granny and me has the key to the storage. She knows I know she know but she won't say she know."

"And she won't. She with us all the way."

"Damn right she is."

"Listen, things is smooth. I see my people once a week and we eat they eat. No one sees me, I see no one. That how we gonna keep it."

"That's a must that we keep it that way."

"So y'all grown soldiers ready to eat with one retired solider and two old ladies?"

"Yes, ma'am."

"Well, like they say in the South, come and get it."

Rudy got up first, smelling the aroma as soon as Granny opened the door with Zack not too far behind. Unc Pete followed them in. Ms. Irene leaned against the wall of the beautiful kitchen, covered with pink and yellow flowered wall paper and cake designer mold makers all on the wall. Rudy couldn't believe his eyes. It was like he was a little boy again. Every one of his favorite foods with there from pork chops, sweet potatoes, collard greens, corn bread, slaw, placed with the homemade lemonade by the plate. The boys and Unc Pete damn near swallow up the whole table eating so fast and thanking Granny and smacking and laughing. These definitely were the good days and more of these were to follow. Granny knew it watching her family. She was very pleased. She held Ms. Irene hand tightly as tears crept down her cheek.

The boys finally full, sat for a minute then said their goodbyes and dropped off Unc Pete and headed back for the barracks. Riding back down the highway to the base, the boys let the breeze blow against them as they reminisced and switched up drivers every now and then until they finally made it to the base. Finally settled in lying in bed that night, Rudy thought about Maryann. How happy he was going to make her, for the rest of her life. He couldn't wait to have a child, boy or girl he would spoil. That's what he was going to do. Marry Maryann, have a child, and spoil the child to death. He smiled as he went into a deep sleep. Zack was adjacent to him snoring really loud.

★★★★★

The days of that week passed quickly with the boys basically training other young pilots on the warfare of the flight game how to win in the air. Zack actually loved the job. Rudy had very little patience. His mind was always somewhere else either on Maryann or his money and his mission to destroy anything in a uniform and that punk azz security guard — he hadn't forgot about him by far.

★★★★★

The weekend came and the boys went to go meet Unc Pete. Unc Pete took them to the stash spot. It was a storage bin that Unc Pete had a lot of his old military belongings in. This place was for veterans only, so it was very unlikely to be searched at any time. The men drove into the place in Unc Pete's old truck. Unc Pete didn't flash at all. Most people thought he was an old solider waiting to die not knowing he was a trained killer with alotta life left in him and alotta drug money stashed and running the heroin through the city on the low. They pulled over and got out the truck. Unc Pete unlocked the door and open the sliding garage door that slid up then walked in the small space through some boxes into the back by a coca cola machine.

"Well here we are boys."

"Is that right?" Zack said as he closed the door.

"That's an old soda pop machine. Where did you get that from?"

"Brought it when I first got out the military in 1968. It never worked. I said was going to get it fixed for years but I knew it would always come in use."

Unc Pete open the side of the machine then hit a button. The back part of it open, displaying shelves on the inside that were lined up with pies of pure opium. 16 to be exact. There it was. Rudy smiled.

"Damn how you put that together, Unc Pete?"

"You know I'm an expert at building shit boy."

"You a mastermind. Damn that's bad. They would never suspect that."

"And it's lined with all kind of deodorizers to prevent any smell at all the dogs can detect. That was the first thing I did."

"Cool. Let's get what we came for and get outta here," said Rudy.

Unc Pete went over and got four pies and put them in a sack and closed the door of the machine and locked it. Then they walked outta the door and got into the truck. Unc Pete drove them back to their car.

"I got it from here boys. Y'all go to back to the barracks. Call me in a few days and we'll be ready."

"'Thanks, Unc Pete. Just take your time."

"Thanks, Unc. See you later and be careful."

This routine was continued bi–weekly, every month, with each receiving their end of the profit. Zack parents had moved up to California. Everything was going good. They had the store transferred to San Leandro at a strip mall so Granny, Ms. Irene and Annie, Zack's mom, were busy. Everyone was happy. Harold found work painting and Zack father helped out at the store.

★★★★★

The year now was 1975 and life couldn't be better. Rudy had worked it out were Rico was going up for an appeal. If everything worked out Rico would get a time cut — a huge one — and be home in no time.

"Damn, it would be good to see old Rico," Zack said.

"Yeah well this lawyer said he would get it done. It might take a little bread but we looking good on the appeal. The judge is a friend of his."

"Shit. Which judges ain't friend of them crooks? All them crooks."

"'You right about that, Zack."

"Say Rudy, we might have to kill that fucking Chief down south. Him and his fucking punk azz cousins."

"What makes you think that?"

"Well I had my peoples check into it and this muthafucka been making alotta phone calls to the feds asking questions bout us."

"Is that right?"

"I don't have to ask. The blonde right?"

"She keeps me informed."

"Why don't you marry her?"

"Man she too clingy. She trying to get transferred here now."

A loud horn began blowing the boys were sitting at the light not knowing it had turned green. The horn kept blowing very loudly. Zack looked back it was a woman. She swirled around them and shot him a middle finger.

"Well I'll be damned."

"Welcome to California."

"Rudy, catch up to that woman. I wanna say something to her."

"Come on, buddy. We gotta go. We don't have time to road rage this morning."

"Nall, I got it."

Rudy speeded up and caught the woman and pulled beside her. Zack got out the car and went to her window tapping on the glass with his hands folded as if he was asking for forgiveness.

"Please, please, baby. Please, forgive." The lady finally turned her head and looked at Zack. She was caught off guard by how handsome Zack was and his well—built frame. She thought in her head, damn that's a man right there. She slowly let down the window.

"Excuse ma'am. My name is Zack. We just got here on your base we here to protect you not hurt you. Let me please make it up to you tonight over dinner." Zack couldn't help but to look down into the car at the beautiful shapely legs the woman had with the blonde hair to match and dimples in her face that made Zack almost melt standing there.

She smiled with a her perfect straight teeth and said, "Why should I go to dinner with you?"

"Because you need to get to know your future husband as soon as possible."

She began to smile even more.

"What's your number and what time will you be ready?"

"How do you know I'm not married?"

"Because I fly jets and have an eagle eye. You have no ring on pretty lady. By the way what's your name?"

"My name is Sarah and I will go only if you are nice and you're not a slow poke like your partner drives."

"That's an agreement."

She reached in her purse and pulled out a paper and wrote her number and address down, as the cars behind her continued to honk their horns.

"Zack, come on man before we get a ticket," Rudy said.

"I will see you later, beautiful."

"Hey what's your name solider?"

"Zack, sweetheart. Zack."

For the next month when Zack was off he spent all his time with Sarah. They were a match made in heaven. She was a divorced woman who worked in a law firm as a paralegal. It wasn't long before Zack had introduced her to the whole family Annie loved Sarah and so did Zack's father. Granny and Ms. Irene thought of her like a niece. Everyone knew it won't be long before they would be hearing wedding bells. Seeing his buddy in love made Rudy wanna marry Maryann even more now. He was on the phone with her everyday grinning and skinning. Life was good.

CHAPTER 8

It was a hot humid day, clear skies, with no wind blowing the average Texas weather in the spring. Even though the sun was going down it was still close to one hundred degrees on the Air Force base outside of Houston. Most of the soldiers were in the barracks cooling off preparing for the next day of a heat filled workday and training. Inside an office of air conditioning sat a master sergeant behind his desk thumbing through some paperwork. His walls were filled with plaques of honors from the war. With his reading glasses resting on his nose, he looked up at the woman sitting across from him.

"You have been a well−disciplined solider doing everything we ask for. I see no reason in not granting your request for transfer. It will be in effect immediately starting tomorrow."

"Thank you so much. Thank you, sir, so much."

"Well you make sure you think about re−enlisting real hard. We need good soldiers like you."

"Yes, sir, I will. And thank you again."

"You're welcome. Have a nice day."

Maryann got up from the chair almost dancing. She had got what she wanted so bad − a transfer to Travis Air Force Base were Rudy was at. She had 4 months left to serve. Rudy only had 3. She wanted to be close to her man. She began packing her things immediately, singing her favorite song as she did.

"I love youuuuuuuuuuuu for so many reasonssssss baby I love youuuuuuuuuuu for all seasons."

"Well somebody feels good tonight I see." It was her bunk mate. She was on her way overseas coming into the military and Maryann was going out.

"I finally got it, girl. I got my transfer. I'm leaving in the morning."

"To see, I know who, Mr. Rudy."

"That's right. I going to get my man."

"Imah miss you, Maryann. You like my big sister."

"I'm only gonna be a phone call and a letter away. You remember what I said and be strong and keep GOD close to you. That's the most important thing."

"Well Imah let you pack. I gotta go shower."

Maryann looked at the young sister as she walked away. She prayed that the young woman would be okay. She was the big sister from a large family that was very poor in Detroit trying to find opportunity in the military. Maryann packed her things up and went and showered. She laid down, fell asleep. The next morning she was looking out the window at the clouds flying high through the sky. She landed at Travis Air Force base around 1:30pm. The flight only took 5 hours with the time change. After getting her luggage, she decided not to call Rudy but to surprise him. Maryann walked through the grounds hoping maybe to spot him without Rudy seeing her but she didn't noticed anyone who resemble him anywhere. She found where she was to report to she decided to go ahead and report in then find Rudy. After getting settled in and finding her sleeping quarters she decided it was time to find Rudy. She called him.

"Hi, baby. what you doing?"

"Hey there, sweetheart. What's up? I was thinking bout you."

"Yeah sure. You probably done forgot bout me that fast."

"Now how can I do that when you always on my mind?"

"Were you at?"

"I'm at the base."

"Where at on the base?"

"Why, what's up? What's wrong?"

"Ain't nothing wrong. I was just wondering where you was at and what you was doing."

"I'm sitting on the lawn just thinking about what my plans our for our future."

"Our future, huh?"

"Yes, ma'am. I was hoping you would join me in a life of happiness and togetherness."

"Is that right?" Maryann said shyly smiling.

"Yes, that's right."

"So, when did you come to this conclusion, sir?" Maryann knew how Rudy felt about her, she just wanted to hear it again as she walked through the grounds trying to find out where Rudy was sitting in the lawn at.

"I been convinced you the one for me every day I'm away from you. Were you at?"

"Hold on baby." Maryann covered the phone up so Rudy couldn't hear the conversation "Excuse me where is the large yard were the soldiers usually relax at after work, sir?" Maryann ask an officer walking past her.

"Go right around the corner you can't miss it, solider."

"Thank you, sir."

"Huh? What did you say?"

Maryann was walking faster now not even noticing it anticipating seeing Rudy.

"Where you at baby and what you doing?"

"I'm always in your heart." There he is, Maryann spotted Rudy as he sat up on the lawn.

He felt something was wrong. She was being crafty with her answers for no reason. "Where you at baby?"

"I'm looking for my man."

"You what?"

Maryann wrapped her arms around Rudy neck and kissed him. He jumped then relaxed. When he realized it was her, he immediately jumped up and hugged her tight, kissing her then hugging her and again then stepped back and just looked at her.

"Damn am I dreaming? Where did you come from? Why you ain't tell me? I would have had things ready."

"I wanted to surprise you. You all I want and need, Rudy. I love you."

"I love you, too Maryann. Never forget that." They began kissing again falling on the grass. It seemed like time had stopped and slow music was playing as they laid there.

"Hey, hey, hey. Get a room, get a room."

They looked up and it was Zack.

"I knew it had to be you, Maryann. I don't know where you came from but I knew my buddy won't be rolling round in the grass like that with no one else but you."

"He better not be."

"You know better than that."

"So sis when you get here?"

"I just got in today."

"Well welcome home. We gotta celebrate tonight. You gotta meet Sarah."

"Who is Sarah?"

"Zack new girlfriend. The boy's in love."

"So are you? So what's wrong with that?"

"Nothing. I just want him to be careful. He just met her but we been knowing each other for like four years now."

"She the one, buddy, I'm telling you."

"Well your sister will find out trust me, brother," Maryann said laughing as they got up and walked towards the buildings.

"Baby, we live down this way. What time will you be ready?"

"I'll be ready in three hours. I will call you." They kissed.

"Ohh, that's so sweet," Zack said laughing.

Maryann walked away. Rudy stood there for a minute and watched her walked away. Damn she was fine.

"Buddy, you a lucky man," Zack said looking at Rudy look at Maryann.

"Yeah, I know it. I know it."

That night they all had a ball. Maryann loved Sarah and she felt the same about her. They painted the town all night long and made it in early that morning. Due to the fact it was a Friday night the gang could hang out very late. So for the next two months the routine was pretty much work during the week and on Friday they would all meet at Granny's house that Maryann adored along with Ms. Irene, learning all the recipes. Having for the last three and a half years here so much about her, it was such warm pleasure to be finally in her presence. It was like she already ready knew them both. On Saturday, the bi—weeks of the month, Rudy and Zack would take a ride with Unc Pete. Maryann and Sarah never paid much attention to it. Looked at it as a boys outing but the whole time they were running their drug ring smoothly with no problems.

★★★★★

Deep in the south sitting behind his desk was Chief Smith fuming mad.

"What do you mean I know they doing something it's no way they can afford that life on the military and a damn fish sandwich store they up to something I know it."

"Well I had my people on them for weeks and they say they just some military boys servicing there country."

"That's some bullshit."

"Well I tell you what, come up with something solid and I'll put more surveillance on them, but as for now we gotta concentrate on other missions."

"Yeah I understand."

The chief hung up slamming the receiver down. He didn't know what they were doing but he was going to find out. Sitting on his desk in front of him was his re—election form. He grabbed it looked at it and then balled it up.

"Fuck this shit. I'm going to California." The chief stormed out his office never to return. That night at home where he lived alone, he called the station and told them him was retiring and later called a travel agency and made arrangements to go to Oakland, California in the near future. He was determined to see them boys in jail.

CHAPTER 9

Natures light was lit brightly in the sky. The birds were singing, the butterflies were lingering through the air as the sun crept over the mountains slowly with the breeze coming in fast from the incoming tide. The sound of water hitting against the rocks could be heard the closer you got to the ocean, but the further you were from it the warmer it got. This was California in the morning. The sound of passing traffic tires rolling across the asphalt was the soundtrack for the business area of downtown San Leandro. Mostly small clothing jewelry, shoe and art shops and restaurants and other small businesses occupied this area. A few auto repairs shops were found here and there but mostly this part of town was for the people visiting their families, people who couldn't wait to move out of the city from the chaos. This was the suburbs of the bay area.

Very few could afford this life. Black people at that were a surprise to see here in this part of town. They were welcomed but a surprise and owning a business was damn near impossible. So Granny's was the talk of the town, a black woman from the south owning her own establishment, couldn't stopped being talked about and her recipes was the hottest item in the kitchen. All throughout the suburbs some women just went to Granny's to hear her talk about how she and Ms. Irene made their dishes. The place was always packed. It was the social spot for women. In no time, no matter the race, in the morning and evenings, everyone had to pass through Granny's.

"Good morning, ma'am. How are you doing?"

"I'm just fine. I heard you have the best fish sandwiches in the world here."

"Well, whoever told you that wasn't lying." Granny said smiling. She no longer had the stock Rudy and Zack daily brought in but she did have her famous breading recipe and the homemade lemonade that no one in miles could mess with. Annie was at the other end of the counter taking care of another customer.

"Well I'll take three of those sandwiches and three lemonades please," the woman said.

"No problem. Be right up."

"Irene, 3 to go, please."

"I got you. Be ready in a second." Ms. Irene didn't like all the paperwork. She liked being in the kitchen so she always took care of the serving. Granny would cook, Ms. Irene would prepare, and they all would count the money at the end of the day. Harold was in the shadows cleaning the tables and coming up with new ideas everyday telling them, "We gotta expand go worldwide. We gotta go worldwide." They would listen but knew they had to lock down this county first.

★★★★★

One evening sitting in Unc Pete's house, Zack and Rudy watched him pull out a suitcase. It had nothing but hundreds in it.

"Damn, Unc Pete. Why don't you put that in a bank?"

"Unlike you boys I never had no way to show where it was coming from."

"You could have said you were an investor in the store."

"Yeah but it's too many of y'all in that bankroll as it is. I didn't wanna cause no suspicion."

"So what you bout to do with all that money?"

"It's gotta be close to a million."

"Damn near half. Damn near half of that." Unc Pete looked up smiling.

"So what's the plan?"

"Well Rudy and Zack you looking at the proud new owner of Pete's Auto Repair. 1015 Market Street."

"Well, I'll be damn Unc Pete. That's alright."

"Yeah, I know. That's what you always talked about so I'm happy for you."

"This is just the beginning. I'm open them all over the city."

The boys shook Unc Pete's hand and they walked out the house, jumped in the jeep and road down the street.

★★★★★

One month later, standing at his bunk smiling was Rudy with his gear in his hand. It was over. The day had come for him to discharge. He looked at the uniform in the locker hanging next to his bunk thinking to himself, now I got they azz. I made it through this bullshit. Now I'm ah get what I be needing all my life — power to destroy whoever is my enemy.

Zack was adjacent to him putting his belongs in his suitcase. "Buddy you bout ready to get outta here?"

"Hell yes. Let's go."

The boys grabbed their things and headed for the door.

"Well, y'all soldiers fight a good one. We did our part," Zack screamed at the top of his voice laughing at the same time.

"Peace fellas," Rudy said and they walked out the door to the jeep and got a ride to the gate where Maryann was waiting.

"Pull over. That's my baby right there," Rudy said.

"Okay, solider."

"Hey there. How you doing?"

"You sneaking out on me, huh? Mr. Rudy. Mr. Civilian."

"By no means. You the prettiest solider I ever seen in my life. I had to see you before I left."

"Why you didn't call me then?"

"I did call. How you think you knew what time to be at the gate? You got the message. I know you did."

"Yes, I did baby and I miss you already."

"Imah call you as soon as I get to Granny's and you coming over this weekend, right? You don't have duty do you?"

"No, I don't." Maryann leaned in and kissed him − something while in uniform was a no no.

"Let me get outta here for I get you in trouble. I'll call you when I get there, baby."

"Okay, baby. Zack, take care of him."

"I will see you this weekend, sis."

"Bye." Maryann stood there thinking about her future with Rudy she only had one month left and her duty was up. She smiled as the jeep pulled off and rolled down the hills and mountains of the western coast passing by the ocean. The highway was packed so it was a pretty much nonstop ride. The driver dropped Zack off first at his moms and dad house in the same neighborhood and then took Rudy to Granny's around the corner from Unc Pete's.

"Thank you very much, solider." Rudy eased out the jeep and grabbed his bags. As he did he handed the solider a few dollars. "The weekends on me."

"No, sir, I can't do that."

"Enjoy yourself and keep your eyes open for me."

He accepted the money from Rudy and drove off. This solider worked in the warehouse on base. He would be very useful in the future.

★★★★★

Sitting on his front porch reading the morning paper, ex−chief Smith was readings the headline. Local Solider Who Saved Many Lives Returns To Civilization Today Discharges From Military As Hero Of War. There was a big picture of Rudy. The ex−chief was fuming at the mouth, so he's a hero huh? Okay. I'm show you a hero. This fucker is a drug dealer and a crook a nigger at that. I'm going to destroy his azz. He grabbed the phone.

"Did you get those addresses I needed?"

"Yes I did," someone on the other end of the phone responded.

"And this Unc Pete of Zack's, do you have all the info on him I needed?"

"We still checking into him and his financial situation now. He ran with a very undisclosed outfit but I have some people that can cut through the red tape."

"So when will I hear from you? How long will all this take?"

"Give me until next week and I should have what you need."

"Thank you."

"Now just remember you owe me a big favor."

"No problem."

The phone went dead as ex—chief smith stared into the sky. Arresting Rudy had become his life now. That's all he had to live for. Wasn't no nigger gonna out smart him, take his family shit, and get rich, and have the whole world thinking he's a fucking hero. Ain't that a bitch. Well Mr. Rudy get ready cause I'm coming for your azz, buddy. The chief leaned back in his rocker and smiled as he sipped on some moonshine, freshly made.

CHAPTER 10

Sitting in the church in the first row was Granny in a lovely long yellow satin ruffled dress. Ms. Irene was next to her in a pink hat with a velvet pink dress to match with a big ribbon on the back of it. Annie was next to her in a green flowered colored dress and white hat to match with a ribbon going around it to match the dress and two sets of some pearls wrapped around her wrist and hanging from her neck. With his arm around his wife proudly, next to her husband who was suited up in a gray double breasted suit with some gray shoes. Unc Pete was sitting there with a cigar in his mouth and a pin stripped suit and hat wearing it like a gangster tilted to the side.

The church was beautiful with tall windows stained with spiritual art, shellacked wooden benches with pretty green cushions in them, soft short shag carpet cover the floor. The roof of the church had gold lamps coming from the ceilings and a large piano sitting where the choir sang behind the pulpit. It was flowers all below the area were the preacher man was standing and also lining the aisles. The seats were all full with smiles and awes on all the people's faces. At each end stood the ushers and the music played softly and slowly. It was wedding day for Zack and Rudy — they were having a double wedding and it was the most beautiful sight to see. Cameras were going off as both grooms walked their brides slowly down the aisle.

A month had pasted quickly Maryann thought and here she was now taking the steps to the rest of her life. She was looking so beautiful with her natural long black shiny hair hanging from her shoulders. The white gown she had seemed to reach for miles behind her. Maryann was blushing, smiling so happy and excited almost bout to cry at the same time. Rudy was in a white tux looking over at her stepping smooth in his white Stacy's Adams. Zack wore all blue also with blue snake skins to go with his suit. Sarah had on a blue pastel dress that stretched quite a distance also down the church aisle. The music continued to play as both couples walked up to the preacher. The cameras began to start clicking to capture the moment. It was definitely love in the air.

The preacher man went through the vows with each couple. He ask them both the magic words and after the I do's was said and the kisses were exchanged, they were off outta the church in limos and headed for the airport. They were out the military now, married and ready to go start their lives.

Sitting on the plane with the girls resting from the long day, the boys exchange hands shakes.

"Yo, the first thang I wanna do is just walk the beach with my girl and look at that pretty clear blue water in Jamaica. I always wanted to come here since I was a little boy," said Rudy.

"Rudy this shit like when Imah wake up. We got a dream life, a fucking dream life, buddy."

"Yeah, it's definitely been going real good."

"Listen, how long we gonna keep on hustling? Though I'm really trying to back outta that shit soon as possible. Shit going too good."

"Well you gotta remember that hustling is what got us here."

"I know. I'm just saying we need to clean up all that loot."

"Yeah you right we do and that punk azz sheriff keep sniffing around. We don't need no setbacks at all."

"I think we should chill for like a six months when we get back. Don't do nothing and go under surveillance our damn selves and see what the fuck is going on for real."

"That might not be a bad idea everybody is ok money wise so we can chill and peep shit and set up legal situations."

"Yeah, I'm also getting kinda scared for Unc Pete. I think the gangster is coming outta him quick. Did you see his outfit at the church?"

"Yeah, he was lucky Luciano for real."

They both started laughing.

"Yeah buddy. We done came too fucking far to let them snatch away what we worked so hard for."

"You ain't ever lied."

"What's on your mind?"

"Strips clubs. X−rated dancers. We can wash alotta money through them joints Rudy, a lot."

"We gonna check into it, buddy. For now, let's enjoy our honeymoons. What you say?"

"You got a deal."

"Zack, you the only brother I got man and ever needed."

"You damn right. Vice versa buddy vice versa."

"What y'all two jabbing about?" Maryann said waking up rubbing her eyes.

Zack leaned over and kissed Sarah on the forehead.

"Oh nothing baby. Just that good old soldier boy talk, that's all."

He kissed her slowly. This man was totally in love with her and she knew it.

The couples spent the next three weeks walking through the lands and hills of Jamaica seeing all the eye could see then dancing their nights away absorbing all the culture of Jamaica they could. It was two days before they were to return to the States. Zack and Sarah were chasing each other up and down the beach in the bare feet. Rudy sat there with Maryann drawing I love you in the sand.

"Baby you know what? It feels good damn good to say I'm your wife."

"Yeah I like now when people ask me who is that like this morning at the store and I told the lady, 'That's my wife.'"

"I heard you. It sounded so sweet too." Maryann put her leg over Rudy's and they continue to draw words in the sand.

"Her name has to be Belize."

"Whose name has to be Belize?"

"Our daughter's."

"Oh so you just know we gonna have a daughter."

"Yes I do. I hope so."

"Why is that?"

"So when you away from me, I can look at her, she a little you, just as pretty an lovely and love me too. I can't lose. I'm have a double scoop of you," he said in a country way that was so romantic. Rudy had a way of doing that Maryann just smiled and hugged him.

"What if it's a boy though?"

"Well you know his name gon be, Rudy."

"I figured that."

"What else?" Rudy said smiling.

"Baby what made you comes up with that name Belize?"

"Look baby." Rudy pointed at a ship passing by slowly. It was so beautiful, long burgundy with yellow thin stripes and small white flowers all over it looking like they were blowing in the wind on the side of it in big letters it said Belize. Maryann looked at her husband and smiled. What more could she ask for? They had been waiting on each other their whole life.

"Baby when we get back, I'm get a job at the postal service and let Granny and Ms. Irene run the store. It will still be income coming in from it for us but I don't wanna come in and seem like I'm taking over you know?"

"I understand. I understand. You might be in for a fight trying to take that place from them ladies."

"Yeah I'm looking for them in a magazine any day. They big celebs up there huh?"

Laughing she agreed.

"What's up with y'all slow pokes? Y'all gonna sit there all day? Let's get our motorbikes and go riding through the hills again." Zack came up holding Sarah hand.

"Zack, you act to dang crazy on that motorbike. You scare me boy."

"I should be scare of you the way you drive Maryann."

They had enjoyed riding early they all were good riders especially Maryann. She was really good having rode them her whole childhood in Tennessee.

"Well, what time you talking bout going?"

"I say we make our way back to the hotel and get ready now."

"Well, let's grab something to eat first. I'm starving."

"Sounds good to me."

"Please no more hot food. I can't take it no more hot spicy food."

"That's all they have over here is spicy food, Sarah."

"Well I'm going to McDonald's. My stomach can't handle no more curry chicken."

They all laughed as they made their way towards the hotel by the beach.

The next two days were spent trying to bottle all this up in a memory taking pictures, going everywhere they thought they hadn't been, and seeing the favorite spots one more time. Finally going to the airport that morning, Maryann couldn't believe it was over and finally it was time to go.

"Baby, you bout ready?" she said to Rudy in the bathroom.

"Yeah call Zack and see if they ready." They were in the suite next door.

"Okay."

"Hello?"

"Good morning, Sarah. How you doing? Y'all bout ready?"

"Maryann, Zack is still fooling with his hair in the mirror. I'm packing this last suitcase. We should be ready in a few minutes."

"Would y'all like to stop and get something to eat or wait till we get to the airport?"

"Nah sister, let's wait till we get to the airport. I don't wanna take no chance of missing our flights."

"Good idea. I'll see y'all in the lobby in a few minutes." Maryann hung up and walked into the bathroom putting her arms around her new husband kissing him slowly on the back of his neck.

"Baby, you ready?"

"Ready for what? You?"

"I know you ready for me. You ready to go?"

"Yeah, well, you gotta be specific walking up on me all sexy like that." He spun around and kissed her and hugged her softly but firmly.

"I love you."

"I love you, too."

★★★★★

One week later, at the real estate office, buying two houses was Rudy and Zack.

"I'm giving you two newlyweds a good deal because I like you guys, and I found you something close by each other also."

"Yes, thank you for that. Thank you very much."

"Yes, thank you again. If we have any questions we have your card. Have a good day, sir."

"You too enjoy your stay and good luck," said the real estate broker.

The boys jumped in their cars and went and got their wives from the hair salon. They had been out house hunting as soon as they got back. Now they were headed for their new homes. The neighborhood was not far from where the rest of the family lived, in the same area. Finally Rudy found it.

As he turned off the main road and made a few more turns into the residential area he made a left into a cul-de-sac. It was only two beautiful homes sitting in the front of them, both were tall brick homes with double garage doors, each had large windows and were two story high with a front and back yard of freshly cut green grass. Shrubbery surrounded the edges of the homes with pools sitting in both back yards along with a wooden deck connecting to the homes.

Maryann and Sarah went right to work decorating the homes. That was all they did for the next two weeks was shop, clean, arrange and rearrange things around the houses.

Meanwhile, Rudy had went to the post office and got a job and Zack was working with Unc Pete helping him run the garage shops — at least the girls thought.

★★★★★

Rudy had left that morning as he usually did with his post office suit on like he was going to distribute mail. It was his uniform, the one he was most proud of. Getting in his car driving to the garage on the eastside like he did every morning, Rudy was listening to the radio as it played Al Green. He sipped on his morning coffee. It was the first real day back to official business. Time to get the rest of these pies off, Rudy thought. Everything was in place now. The family was straight business, they were out that military bullshit he thought, so now let's get this retirement money. Ten pies left, baby, ten pies left.

"So how everything been going Unc Pete since we left?"

"You know they been calling. I told them to relax awhile."

"Well let's crank it back up cause that fucking wedding and honeymoon and house done bout broke my azz."

"What you ain't enjoy it?"

"Yeah but my money gone. I didn't realize we was spending so much money."

"Well we always got the businesses."

"I'm just saying buddy. I liked when my money was stacked. Let's stack some more."

"Well they definitely ready. They been waiting for y'all to say when."

"Well make the call. Set it up. We only got ten left."

"Fuck, we need to go get some more, Rudy."

"Nah. We need to stack all this paper and we out buddy. That's was the plan."

"Yeah stick to the plan. It getting dangerous real dangerous out in these streets."

"What's going on?"

"Murders, robberies, under covers. It's best to get what you can and get the fuck out this game. Retire and wash the money."

"And that's what the businesses is for right?" Zack said.

"That's right Zack."

"Well I tell you what, along with what we got we getting some strip clubs they always make money."

"Okay, buddy, whatever you want."

"Hell, you just wanna see the girls, Zack. That's all boys," said Unc Pete.

"Yeah so set that up and let us know when."

"I got you, Rudy." Rudy hugged Unc Pete and so did Zack. The boys walked down the stairs out the garage and got into Zack's truck. It looked like a regular old pickup truck. Rudy drove a family car to work but had a brand new caddy in the garage and also one that Maryann drove around town in. Zack like older hot rods — he had a 67 impala stocked in the garage at home.

"So you wanna open some strip clubs, huh?"

"Hell yeah. Its alotta money go through them joints."

"Sounds like a winner to me, buddy. Check into it."

"Listen we just gonna stack this money and invest it."

For the next three months Zack and Rudy had the same routine coming and going to work, meeting with Unc Pete and getting the pies off. Everything was going as planned. On the weekends they took the girls out to where ever they wanted to or sat around Granny's house watching movies and eating and laughing all night long. Life was good.

They were at Granny's this particular evening.

"I've been feeling real sick, Granny. I throw up twice this morning."

"I saw it when you walked in, baby, but I wasn't sure. I was gonna ask you later."

"Ask me what?"

"You ready to be a momma?"

"Aye what?"

"A momma, cause you pregnant Maryann."

"How you know? I was going tell you I am feeling funny."

"Listen baby when a woman skin shining like that and she just got married it ain't hard not to tell."

They both hugged each other and laughed Maryann thought about how she and Rudy couldn't stop making love since they had got back. She was going straight to the doctor in the morning.

"Well Granny don't say nothing to Rudy till I go to the doctor in the morning please."

"I won't child. I'll let you tell him."

The boys were out in the back yard talking.

"Y'all come in and eat. The food is ready," said Ms. Irene.

"Guess what Maryann's pregnant?"

"I thought I told you don't say anything."

"Oh that's just Irene."

"What you mean just Irene?"

"No, she don't want Rudy to know till she sho, that's all. But I know. Look can't you tell, Irene?"

Ms. Irene looked at Maryann. "Umm uh. She sho is," she said and hugged Maryann.

"What y'all in here grinning about?"

"All nothing, Rudy. Come on and let's eat."

The ladies continued to laugh.

★★★★★

The next morning inside an office sitting on the couch reading a magazine was Maryann. She was waiting on her results from her test.

"The doctor said she will be right with you Miss."

"Thank you." Maryann continued to try to read the magazine as she thumbed through it but she was nervous. Why they were taking so long?

"Hello Ms. Jones. Your results came back."

"Yes?"

"You will be a mother in eight months. Congratulations!"

"Thank you, thank you! I'm so happy, thank you." Maryann began crying. She immediately went to the phone and called Rudy and told him the good news. Then she called back home to her parents and told them. They were really happy. Maryann had been trying to get her parent to come to California but they hadn't been able to come out yet. She promised her mom that she would bring the baby home as soon as it was born, if they hadn't come out to California by the time the baby was born.

Months passed like days. It seemed like for some reason Sarah had been acting real strange and Zack was becoming real irritated with her. Maryann and her had got into an argument. It was something Sarah was holding from Zack about her past and she won't tell him. She had started drinking heavy and hanging out in bars more at night. Maryann tried to explain that wasn't good for their marriage she didn't seem to see nothing wrong in it.

Maryann was 5 months pregnant now so she stayed at home a lot. She got a call from Sarah one night.

"I can't do it no more. I can't do it."

"What's wrong, Sarah?"

Rudy sat up in bed looking at his wife holding the phone.

"Zack wants a son. He wants a son. Zack wants a son."

"What Sarah were you at?"

"Zack wants a son and I can't give him one. I can't have no kids."

Since the announcement of Maryann being pregnant that's all Zack had talked about. His new baby boy. He joked around the family how him and Sarah would be the next to be having a family.

Sarah sat in the drive way of her home. That was all she could think of with the windows of her car down the night air on her face crying hysterically in the phone. The lights of the house were out. It didn't look like Zack was home yet but maybe he was sleep, she thought. She hadn't open the garage yet.

"Sarah, Sarah are you okay?"

"No I'm not. I don't know what to do."

"You have to tell him."

"Tell him I can't have kids cause I was a prostitute and got raped?"

Maryann almost dropped the phone. "You can't hide nothing from him. Zack loves you y'all can adopt children."

"He wants his blood son. That's all he talks about, his son. To be what his dad wasn't to him."

"Where are you at right now?"

"I'm at home bout to go in the house." Head lights came into her rear view mirror it was Zack. "Zack just pulled in. I gotta go."

Maryann looked at the receiver as it went dead and turned to Rudy. "Don't ever keep no secrets from me, do you promise?"

"What's wrong with you?"

"Do you promise?"

"Yes." Not really thinking bout what he said at the time.

"What happen? What's going on with Sarah?"

"She's been lying to Zack about her past. She was a prostitute and got raped and now cause of that she can't have kids."

"Damn, that ain't good. He gonna flip."

"You think so?"

"I know so. She should have just told him the truth."

"Yeah that's why I said don't hold no secrets from me, Rudy. Ever."

Rudy looked at her. The only thing he didn't tell her was about the pies and they would be gone soon. They were getting closer every day to getting outta the game.

The door of Zack Truck slammed shut and he walked up to Sarah's car door she was trying to wipe away the tears from her eyes.

"Hey, baby."

"Hi hi Zack," she said, kinda drunk through her teary voice.

"What's wrong with you?"

"Zack, I need to tell you something."

"What?" He opened the car door and got close to her. He had suspected that she was cheating on him. "What? What do you need to tell me?"

"Zack, I can't."

"You can't what?"

"I can't have no kids. When I was young a was making street money and got raped and I can't have no kids."

"You was a ho."

"I had to do wat I had to do."

"You didn't have to lie to me about it though. You made me look like a fool and lied to me knowing I wanted a son. Why you ain't tell me?"

"I didn't know how to. I'm sorry. I'm sorry."

"I can't trust you no more. How I know you ain't been lying about everything else you been telling me hanging out all night?"

"Zack, that's why I been drinking. It was driving me crazy. You know I don't mess around on you."

"How the fuck I know that?"

"Why are you cussing me?"

"Cause you a lying bitch and I don't love you no more."

"What? You don't love me?"

"Fuck nah. I don't love you get the fuck outta my house."

"This my house too."

"Bitch." Zack leaned in and smack her. Sarah clawed at his face scratching him all in his eyes. Zack tried hard to get the wildcat he knew as his wife off of him. Finally he pushed her away.

Rudy and Maryann heard the commotion and came out side and separated the two of them. Maryann escorted Sarah in the house as Rudy tried to calm down his friend. He was trying to stop her from going in the house.

"That bitch ain't staying here!"

"Buddy listen to me. Calm down, calm down. Don't say nothing you will regret."

"Fuck that. She getting her lying azz outta my life. I don't trust no liars."

Rudy looked at his friend and saw the seriously in his eyes and heard it in his voice. Zack was through with her.

Sarah said, "Maryann what the hell am I supposed to do? What am I supposed to do?"

"Just give him some time. He will come around."

"He smacked me. He smacked me. I'm afraid of what he might do to me. He will never forgive me. I know he won't."

"Lord has mercy."

"What am I going to do?" Sarah began crying and grabbed Maryann by the shoulders. Maryann looked up and there was her husband looking at them standing in the doorway.

Zack sitting on the steps with his face in his hands not believing what had just happen to his life.

"Tell Zack I will leave. I don't wanna be no where I ain't wanted."

"Good get the fuck out then," Zack screamed over Rudy's shoulder. He was now standing beside Rudy looking into the house.

"I will you can have this shit. Fuck you too, Zack, fuck you too." Sarah ran upstairs and began putting things in a bag. Maryann went behind her as fast as she could.

Zack went over to the couch and sat down. Rudy followed him not really knowing what to say to his buddy.

"You know what Rudy? Ain't no woman ever gonna do that to me again."

"She made a mistake."

"That was a big mistake. She couldn't trust me to love her unconditionally?"

"She probably was scared."

"Fuck that shit. I can never trust her again."

"So what you gonna do?"

"What you mean? That bitch is leaving. I'm okay."

"Maybe you should give it some time."

"Fuck that. What Imah do is stack like you said and be single with strip clubs everywhere and get rich. That's what I'm gonna do. This bitch taught me a lesson. Don't trust'um."

Sarah walked down the stairs crying holding a few bags. She got to the door and turned. "Zack, I'm sorry. I do love you. I hope you forgive me. I'm going to get a lawyer. I won't fight your divorce if that's what you want."

"Yep that's what I want. A divorce from you immediately. ASAP."

"Bye Maryann. Good bye Rudy," Sarah said crying as she close the door and got in her car and left.

One month later they met at a lawyer's office downtown and signed the divorce papers. It was official. They were now over with.

That night Zack negotiated his first venture as a strip club owner, signing the papers, getting the deed to the building. The grand opening of UNCLE PETES TREATS would be in sixty to one hundred twenty days Zack couldn't wait.

CHAPTER 11

It was a late night at the hospital. Maryann had been there all day. The contractions were coming faster and faster. Granny was sitting there with her holding her hand. Rudy was in the waiting room asleep. He had been there for the last three hours. When he wasn't pacing the floor in the room worrying everybody concerned about Maryann, and the baby the nurses finally got him to go to the lobby and relax.

"Granny, Granny I think it's coming. I think he's coming."

"Ohh my goodness, child hold on." Granny stood up and hit the button for the nurses. You could hear the feet coming down the hall. They were on their way.

"Granny, please get someone. It's hurting. It's hurting."

Maryann cried out awaking Rudy. He jerked from the sound of her voice and bolted into the room.

"What's wrong? What wrong, Granny?"

"Ain't nothing wrong. She's having the baby."

"Oooohhhh oooohh!" Maryann let out.

"Baby, you okay. Hold on. Breathe."

"Excuse me, sir, you are going to have to wait outside. Please, sir," the nurse said to Rudy ushering him back out to the lobby as she closed the curtains behind her.

"Granny, ohhh, Granny it hurts."

"Hold on, baby, hold on. It want be long now."

"Ma'am, you will need to step aside and put on a facial mask if you are going to be in here."

"Yes, I understand. I understand." Granny grabbed a facial mask one of the nurses were handing her.

The nurses gathered around Maryann bed and prepared her for delivery. Within a few minutes and hollering from Maryann the sound of a loud cry from the baby could be heard in the room and it reached the lobby.

Rudy heard it and ran in past the nurses. "That's my baby. Let me see. Let me see."

The nurses couldn't hold Rudy back as he got close to the bed one of them handed him a facial mask and tied it on him.

"It's a girl, Rudy, it's a girl," Granny said smiling.

Maryann was looking up at him. The nurses were wiping the new born baby off. They finished and handed her to Rudy. He was all teeth.

"Hey little princess. Hey there. How you doing baby girl?"

Maryann started crying. The look she saw in Rudy eyes was something of a dream. He loved this little baby already.

"So what's her name Rudy?" said Granny.

"Belize. My baby name is Belize."

After all the fanfare Granny finally got Rudy to leave. Granny stayed the night with Maryann just in case. Plus she wanted to hold her great granddaughter as long as she could.

Rudy went to the house and talked Zack to sleep about what he was gonna do for Belize. Zack was awarded Unc god father. He was happy couldn't wait to see his niece.

Within the next week Maryann was home with Belize. The house was completing different now. Everything had to be extra sanitized. Everything went on the baby's time between Granny, Ms. Irene, and Zack's mom, Annie, Maryann had to fight for time with her daughter. She was the apple of everyone eye, such a little darling with the prettiest eyes and jet black her you ever seen. Dark completion like Maryann – rich, chocolate, dark, mahogany–like color.

Nine months later Belize was tearing down everything she could get her hands on. She was a very active little baby.

★★★★★

Earlier one morning inside Unc Pete garage, the boys sat there with him as usual.

"Well we almost done with these pies, Unc."

"Yep two more to go."

"So, what you thinking about, Zack?"

"Honestly, I really thought this shit would never end."

"What you mean?"

"I been kinda waiting on something bad to happen."

"Don't even think that way."

"All this shit been too good to be true."

"Shit we worked hard for what we got. Took chances and they paid off. It's the America way."

"Yeah well let's wrap this shit up. Wash this last load and we done."

"Sounds good to me."

"Well y'all ready?"

The boys and Unc Pete went to their usual stash spot, got what was needed, and Unc Pete handled it from there.

"I'll give you a call when I'm ready," said Unc Pete.

"Okay Unc. Talk to you later."

The boys pulled off and Unc Pete went on to handle the business.

Rudy went straight home. He couldn't wait to go play with Belize. Zack headed to the building going over improvements for the designs of the club.

Back at the house, Granny had Belize on her lap talking to her like she was an adult and it seemed Belize understood everything she was talking about clearly amazingly, to be only nine months.

"So, what you wanna be when you grew you pretty lady?"

Belize looked up smiling with no teeth.

Granny picked her up and tickled her. Their days were spent together having Granny reading to her children books and playing music. Granny said it was important for a baby to have certain kinda sounds around them early. It helped them to develop their sense of sound so she always had music playing soundly in the room with Belize and Belize often sat by the speaker and rocked in rhythm to the grooves of the music as Granny hummed along. This delighted Granny and amazed Maryann and Ms. Irene they couldn't believe it.

A year and a half past quickly. Little Belize was getting bigger everyday. Her hair was long and curly usually in braids going down her back. She tried to talk her tale off. She stay in something always wanting to help.

One day Rudy brought home a small guitar. She went crazy. That night her and Granny sat by the speaker and she mimicked the sounds coming out of the speaker. Every day you could find her by that speaker trying to play whatever she heard coming outta the speaker.

Her mother stood back and watch her baby girl and just smiled. She was a good girl never crying a lot. She stay happy, she was a happy baby. Rudy spoiled her to death. All he did was bring her something home every day. She had more toys that the toy store in her room which had just been changed to a look like a music studio. It had music notes, drums, guitars, and pianos painted all on the walls. Belize had seen it on TV and went into a fit pointing so Maryann got her room painted like that. When Rudy would come home after giving her her surprise for the day, he would take her to the basement and wrestled with her, show her little moves, teaching her balance all this.

Maryann didn't know she thought it was there quiet time or something. One day she walked in on them.

"Hey what are you teaching my daughter?"

"Only balance only balance."

"That ain't no balance. That's karate, Rudy."

"It will help her dance baby. Ain't no harm in it."

She smiled she could see the love in the father's eyes for their daughter. She walked back up the stairs on the phone.

"Momma I will send you more pictures, I promise." Maryann still hadn't had a chance to make it back home and neither had her parents had the chance to come there but they got pictures of Belize every week.

Maryann was supposed to plan a trip home soon. Something always happen though time went fast.

Belize was now three years old and her birthday coming up. She was playing the guitar like it was born on her hand and catching on to the guitar fast.

"Momma, I'm a star," said Belize riding with her mother to the store holding on to her guitar.

"Yes, you are little girl."

"What song you want me to sing?"

"Sing my favorite."

She began singing Al Green 'Let's stay together' and playing on her guitar almost in correct tune.

"Hey that's pretty good." Maryann was amazed by the talent of her little girl. She knew it was big things ahead for her. You could see it. She was ahead of her time. Belize continued to entertain her mom as they drove on.

She looks and swears she sees Zack truck pass her with Rudy in it. She looks in her rearview mirror and it was Zack so Maryann makes a U-turn thinking, let me stop Rudy and see if he wants to go to lunch with us.

Rudy and Zack pulled into a restaurant and go inside and meet Unc Pete. As they were coming out two men approached them. It was the local narcs. They had been following them.

"Excuse me gentlemen. San Leandro Narcotics. Can we see what you have in that bag sir?" one of the officer said as both of them flashed their badges and with guns in their hands.

"What's the problem?"

"Just hand over the bag."

Rudy knew he was stuck. He was thinking were is Unc Pete?

"Are we under arrest?"

The officer lifted up their guns and pointed at both Zack and Rudy.

"Put your fucking hands in the air and drop the bag now." The officer clicked his weapon.

Rudy and Zack put their hands in the air and Rudy dropped the bag.

"Stay in the car." Maryann had pulled over she jumped out the car and ran over to the scene.

"What's is going on? What is going on?" Maryann now right by the officer demanding an answer.

"Back up— misses back the fuck up," one officer said screaming.

"That's my husband. That's my husband."

"Well your husband is doing some dirty work. Where did he get all that money from?" The officer had dumped the bag out on the hood of a car. There had to be more than 100,000 on the hood and it had their two guns the feds had founded on them.

"We own business. What is going on?"

"Your husband and his buddy are under investigation. I suggest you get a lawyer and meet us downtown."

They lead Rudy and Zack away and out came Unc Pete handcuffed by a another officer who had came from the back.

"What! Wait a minute you can't just arrest them like that. What did they do?"

"They have alotta cash money on them. That's enough for now." He walked away from Maryann and got into his car.

"Baby, go to Granny's and call my lawyer."

"Okay." Maryann ran back to the car got in and started it.

"What they doing to my Daddy, Momma?"

"It's a mix up. We going to Granny house to straighten it out."

"Where they going, Momma?"

"Baby sit back." She reached over and put the seat belt on Belize and pulled into traffic and headed fast for Granny's house.

★★★★★

Rudy looked at Zack in the back of the car next to him.

"Don't say nothing till we with our lawyer."

"Got you." Zack nodded.

"Shut up back there. You boys in alotta trouble," the driver said continuing to weave in and outta traffic headed to the federal downtown building.

★★★★★

Maryann pulled into Granny's driveway opening the door at the same time she put the car in gear.

"Come on baby get out the car." Maryann looked back and Belize was getting out the car. Maryann ran to the door knocking on it again and again till Granny open it with her mouth open.

"What's wrong? What's going on, Maryann? Why you knocking like that?"

"They arrested Rudy, Zack, and Unc Pete!"

"They what?"

"They arrested them! I was taking Belize to the store and I saw Rudy so I turned around and when I got there they had them in handcuffs."

"What?"

"Baby, come on in here," Ms. Irene said to Belize.

"They founded a bunch of money and guns on them."

"Ohh lord not again."

"Not again? What you mean, Ms. Irene?"

Granny looked at Irene "We need to call the lawyer."

"Yeah that's what Rudy said. Call the lawyer."

Granny went over and dialed his number "Hello?"

"Yes this is Rudy grandmother. How you doing? We have a problem they just arrested my grandson."

"How you doing, Granny?"

"I don't know. They arrested Rudy."

"Just calm down. Let me make a call."

"Let me speak to him." Granny handed Maryann the phone. She told him what had happen.

"Well they young men that's successful in California and they do have somewhat of a past so that's why they being harassed."

"A past? What you mean? They just discharged from the military."

The lawyer then realized that maybe he had said too much.

"Let me make this phone call. I'll get this straighten out. I will call you right back." He hung up.

"Granny, what is the lawyer talking bout Rudy's past?"

Granny looked at Irene and Irene lowered her head.

"What is going on, Granny? What are they talking bout?" Belize sat there eyes wide open.

"Honey, Rudy and Zack were in some trouble a few years ago down south and they had to go to the military or jail."

"In trouble for what?"

"Drugs and guns and a police murder by Rudy's cousin Rico who is in jail right now."

"Oh my God. Why ain't nobody tell me all this."

"I mean they were young boys then."

"Well evidently they haven't stopped."

"We don't know what happen, Maryann. Let's calm down."

"I can't believe this. I been living a lie the whole time. I been living with a gangster." She went over and hugged Belize who was just looking around the room.

"Maryann, Rudy ain't a bad boy. Him and Zack were good children. They got into that one thang that was it and they never proved they were doing what they accused them of anyway."

"Well you can sit back and not think so but I knew it was not just military money we was living off of and where did the money come to the start the business tell me that?"

"Just calm down, Maryann, calm down."

"Ain't nobody say my boys was angels but they good boys," Granny said.

Maryann came over and hugged Granny along with Belize. "Granny I didn't mean anything by what I said. I'm sorry. I'm sorry."

The phone rang.

Granny picked up the phone "Hello, hello."

"Yes, Granny." It was the lawyer. "The boys are under investigation for money laundering. They holding them for 72 hours but they will be released. It's just a formality."

"But what they charged with?"

"Nothing as of yet."

"They trying to seize all financial records. They getting a warrant for that now."

"Well when will they be home?"

"Like I said in 3 days. Don't worry I got this under control, Granny. They have nothing but suspicion."

"Okay thank you so much. I will call you in two days. Good night."

Granny told everyone what the lawyer said. "Maryann do you know the accountants number?"

"Yes."

"You need to call him in the morning. We need to set up a meeting with him."

"Irene go call Annie and let her know what's happen. Tell her we meeting with the accountant tomorrow."

"So what we about to do, Granny?"

"We bout to make sure all the paper work is correct. They about to audit us. I know."

"This is all crazy."

"I'm taker my baby home. I will see y'all tomorrow."

"Bye, Granny. Bye, Ms. Irene," Belize said walking out the door not smiling knowing something was wrong.

On the way driving home Maryann thought to herself that she had been betrayed to, lied to, by the one man she had gave her all to, her life to. She didn't know if she could trust him again.

Maryann pulled in the driveway and walked in the house. She put Belize to sleep and lay in her bed thinking.

The next morning she sat at the breakfast table eating cereal with Belize.

"How would you like to go see your grandma in Memphis and all your cousins?"

"Can Daddy come?"

"Yes. he will come later."

"Okay. When?"

"I'm find out right now." Maryann picked up the phone and began dialing. She called down south to Memphis. "Hello, hello, hello."

"Yeah mama, it's Maryann. What you doing?"

"Hello Maryann, that you girl?"

"Yeah it's me."

"It's good to hear your voice, child. How you been doing?"

"I been okay," she said beginning to cry.

"Baby, what's wrong?" her mother said, hearing it in her voice.

"Mama, I need to come home for a while."

"What's wrong child?"

"Nothing. I just miss home."

"Well you come on home. I wanna see my grand baby anyway. When you coming?"

"We leaving tonight."

"We leaving," Belize said and ran out the room.

"Yeah I'm book the flight and call you back later. Bye. I love you, mama."

"I love you too, baby. See you when you get here."

"Belize. Belize. Belize?"

"I don't wanna a go! I don't wanna go! I wanna see my daddy! I wanna see my daddy!"

"You will see him baby. He coming later I promise. Okay?"

"Momma, you promise?"

"I promise."

"Can we go see Granny before we leave?"

"Uhhh yesss we can we can go see Granny before we leave. Now go upstairs and take your clothes out your drawer for mama and put them on your bed."

★★★★★

Within a few hours the flight was booked, clothes were packed and Maryann was walking out the door the phone rang. "Hello?"

"Hey baby how you doing?" It was Rudy. Maryann held the phone in shock. She wasn't expecting to hear from him.

"Why did you lie to me Rudy?"

"Lie to you? What you talking about?"

"The drugs and guns and money. What you think I'm talking about?"

"Baby listen. I don't know what you talking about. These people is crazy I need you to come and see me." Rudy couldn't say nothing over the phone incriminating himself so he played like he didn't know what Maryann was talking about.

"Well I'm leaving. Me and the baby going to Memphis. I need to think. I don't know who you are."

"Why you leaving? I need you."

"You should have been honest with me Rudy."

"Baby I was. Please don't leave."

"We gone tonight. I can't be around you, none of this right now. I'm taking my baby somewhere safe."

"What you mean safe?"

"They talking bout audits and what next?"

"You panicking. Listen this is nothing a mistake. We coming home in a day or so."

"It don't matter. You lied to me. I don't trust you no more."

The phone went dead and Maryann hung up and walked out the door. She looked down at Belize and grabbed her hand.

"Come on baby." They close the door and walked to the car got in and sped off headed to Granny's house.

*****

"That's it. phone time is up for tonight," the officer said standing next to Rudy as he held the receiver in his hand in disbelief. Rudy walked back to his cell and laid down. Damn, he thought, she done left me and took my baby.

*****

"Granny, I just need to get away for a while breathe for a minute."

"When do you plan on coming back?"

"I don't know right now. But I will be back."

"Well you grown. I can't stop you. You know we love you and Rudy does too."

"Yeah, I'm not sure who Rudy is right now though."

"Quit that foolish girl. Maryann he just tried to give his family a good life. That's all he ever talked about. Just remember that baby."

"Irene this all is so crazy. I got a lot to think about."

"Come mere baby. You know I'm miss you."

"I'm miss you too, Granny."

Belize hugged Granny crying and then went and hugged Ms. Irene/

"You better call me every day little girl."

"Yes ma'am. I will. I promise."

"Well I will call you when I get there."

"What do I tell Rudy when he calls?"

"I spoke to him, he knows. He called right when we was leaving. Goodbye." Maryann walked out the door holding Belize hand and got into her car and drove straight to the airport.

A federal agent was sitting across the street watching her pull away.

★★★★★

"Hello, Chief Smith how you doing country boy?"

"Is this who I think it is?"

"It sure is and I got some good news for you."

"Well lay it on me."

"I thought about what you said bout them boys and put another lead on them come to find out his Unc Pete runs a garage and a lot of Pete's old military buddies are doing damn good off what Unc Sam left them which wasn't much. When we looked into it a little bit further, we realized them old birds were moving something through underground, weapons and drugs we suspect. All we got for now is a bunch of untraced money and unlimited front money for businesses they run. They got to explain that to the I.R.S. That's where we come in Smith."

"Shit that's the best news I heard all day. I'm on my way to California first thang, smoking."

See you when you get here buddy."

The sheriff jump off his couch not having moved that fast in a long time. He gather his stuff and packed in a suitcase and headed out the door to the airport smiling, thinking, we got your azz now buddy.

CHAPTER 12

The south was a welcome change for Maryann; the fresh smell of nature in the morning, no smog, the sounds of bees buzzing and birds chirping reminded her of her childhood. As she sat under a big tall pine tree thinking of her last years spent in love with Rudy, of Belize and everyone in California.

"Hi child what you doing out here?" her mother asked her.

"I wasn't doing nothing momma just thinking."

"Well you know life comes with ups and down you gotta just keep your faith in GOD."

"I feel like I don't know who the man is I fell in love with."

"From what I understand Rudy is a good man Maryann."

"Yeah but why did he lie to me about his past?"

"Baby I don't have the answer for that. The question is do you love him?"

"Yes I do but I had plans of working for the FBI and how can I do that with a gangster for a husband?"

"Baby things will work out just pray on it."

"Well I'm taking the exam next week for the FBI and I'm not letting nothing stop me from that love or no love."

Belize came running out the back door greeting them both.

"Hey Momma, hey Grandma."

"Hey pretty lady what you doing?"

"I'm go play my guitar." Belize had been playing her guitar every day since she got back nonstop. She was such a pretty little girl; long black hair like her mother and dimples to match with the cutest smile you ever seen. The next week, sitting in a room full of desks and attentive students was Maryann taking her exam for the FBI. It took two hours but when she walked outta the room she knew he had passed it, she wouldn't find out for the next six months. Time passed fast and as it did Maryann just sat around the house and watched her daughter grow. Everyday Belize would be on the phone talking to Granny in California and her father who she missed so much. Finally, Maryann got the letter she was accepted into the FBI she would be leaving in two weeks for training. Sitting at the table looking at Belize she was deciding what she should do, let Belize stay here or go back to California.

"Baby Momma has to go to Washington DC for training for my new job will you stay with Grandma and be good while I'm gone baby?"

"Yes Momma I will."

Belize was going on four years old now getting bigger by the days. During the next four years Maryann travel back and forth from Washington to Tennessee. Belize was going on nine now and excelling in school never gave anyone trouble. She was a good girl everyone loved her, she stood out in music class and even was starting to play basketball as good as some of the boys at school. The summer rolled around and Rudy had been begging Maryann to let Belize come back to California he hadn't seen his daughter in five years finally she agreed.

★★★★★

Back in California the past five years Rudy and Zack were laying low and running the strip club which was now in full force. The feds seemed to be off their case but it was far from that, they were watching them waiting on a mistake.

★★★★★

Sitting at the airport with her Grandma and Maryann Belize looked around the big place with all the planes landing and taking off.

"Momma when I grow up I'm buy you one of them planes so we can go see Daddy whenever we want to."

"That's nice baby."

"What about me?" Grandma said.

"You gonna be with us Grandma always."

The call came for Belize's flight. Maryann walked her daughter to the gate and hugged her tightly before she entered the ramp way leading to the plane.

"Baby be good on the plane and have your Daddy call me as soon as you get there okay?"

"Okay Momma."

"I love you, baby."

"I love you too Momma and you too Grandma." She hugged both of them. Within minutes she was in the air flying thru the sky. Belize fell into a sleep and was awoken by the screeching of the wheels landing in Oakland airport. She was there. The stewardess helped her off the plane and walked with her to the entrance of the gate. There he was waiting with Zack. Belize took off running into her Dad's arms.

"Daddy! Daddy! Daddy!"

"Hey baby. Dang you done got big."

"Is that all you see is your Daddy?"

"Hey Uncle Zack." She hugged him.

"So you remember me huh?"

"Yes." Belize said smiling.

"Well let's go get your bags and get outta here."

They walked to baggage claim Belize holding her Daddy's hand the whole way.

"Daddy when can I move back home when you and Momma not gonna be mad at each other no more."

"Baby Imah talk to your Momma about that. Hopefully you can stay out here and go to school this year."

"For real I can?"

"If I can get your Momma to say yes, you can."

"When you gonna ask her?"

"Wait till you get settled in first okay?"

"Okay daddy."

"Do you see your bags yet?"

"There they are, right there, Daddy. There they are."

Rudy grabbed the bags and they walked through the airport and got into the car.

"Daddy this is a pretty car. I like it. What kind is it?"

"It's a Cadillac, baby."

"It's bad."

"Yeah I work hard for what I have baby, very hard."

"Can I ask you something daddy?"

"What's that?"

"Why are you and Momma mad at each other?"

Rudy looked up in his rearview mirror at Zack.

"Well baby you old enough to know what's going on. I never wanna lie to you. That's why me and your Momma ain't together now."

"What do you mean?"

"Well when I was young me and your uncle Zack got into some trouble and had to go to the military or go to jail and I never told your Momma about it. She found out and got mad and took you to Tennessee."

"What did you and Uncle Zack do Daddy?"

Rudy looked up in his rearview mirror again. "We were selling drugs."

"Drugs. Why did y'all do that daddy?"

"In America, you need money to survive, to live. I wanted my family to have the best so I did what I had to do."

"Did you kill someone?"

Rudy look in the rearview again "No baby I didn't but if I had to I would to protect my family."

"Well if they mess with you, they mess with me. We fighting them together."

"You know how to fight?"

"Yeah them boys at school don't bother me. They know I can fight good."

"How they know that?"

"Cause one day after school this boy was messing with me and I punched him in the mouth and he ran."

"Does your Momma know about this?"

"No I didn't tell her."

"Yeah I think we better keep it a secret okay?"

"Okay."

Rudy turned into Granny's driveway and parked the car. Sitting on the front porch was Ms. Irene and Granny.

"Look at who's waiting on you."

Rudy rolled down the window. "Hey there ladies what's going on?" said Rudy.

Granny and Ms. Irene looked up smiling.

"Daddy I don't wanna go back down there. I wanna stay with you."

"Baby like I said, we gotta ask your Momma about that."

That summer went by fast. Everyday Belize would ride around with her Daddy then go to karate class then go to Granny's house. She learn how to sew and cook she was having a ball. Uncle Zack had took her out fishing and taught her how to fish and he even let her shoot his rifle. She didn't wanna leave.

Finally it was time to go home. Belize cried over the phone until her Mother promise to let her come back the next summer.

For the next three years Belize would come to California for the summer and it was like going to a different school for her. She learned so much in such a short time. She was going on twelve now, really getting big and starting to blossom into a young woman. She was developing.

Back out in California on one of her summer visits, Belize and Rudy were rolling through the city in his new Caddy he had just brought right before she came. He was bumping Al Green, her favorite music.

"Baby, I want you to always remember something. Don't nobody in this world owe you nothing. You gotta get out here and make it happen."

"Daddy, do you still sell drugs?"

"No, I don't baby but if I had to feed you I would."

"Why do people use drugs?"

"Because life has pressures that comes with it. Some people try to hide from the pressure through drugs."

"Well I don't want you to sell drugs no more. They might put you in jail but even if you do, I will still love you, Daddy."

"Thank you, baby."

"Imah be a star so we never have to worry bout nothing no more. I'm buy you whatever you want, Daddy."

"That's what I'm talking bout. Well you just keep working hard and it will happen and stay away from them boys."

"What boys? I don't like no boys."

"Yeah but one day you will. Just remember all they wanna do is get in your pants. That's all."

"Daddy I don't have time for them. They stink anyways."

Rudy started laughing. He knew it won't be long before she changed her mind.

"Maybe one day me and your mother will be together again but until then don't never be afraid to tell us what's going on. No matter what it is baby do you understand?"

"Yes I do."

"I been listening to your sing and rap. I really think you got what it takes."

"You like it daddy?"

"Yes I do."

"Just remember, ain't no one in this world like you. Never forget who you are, a born star, baby, a born star."

"I won't."

"And don't take no jive from no one. I don't care who they are. Listen I got some good news for you."

"What's that, Daddy?"

"I talked your Momma into letting you stay out here for school this year."

"For real Daddy for real?"

"Yup so you gotta keep them grades up and be good so she might let you stay longer."

"I am. Don't worry I am."

"Baby let me ask you something. Do your Momma have a boyfriend?"

"No she always talking about her job and stuff. I don't think so."

"Do she ever talk about me?"

"No not really."

"Uhhh."

"One time though she was crying holding the wedding picture of y'all. I think she still in love with you."

"I really hope so. I do miss her. I do."

★★★★★

Belize did real good in school that year, even improving on her grade point average and joining the band and choir. Also she was starting on the girls basketball team. She was so good the coach begged Maryann to let her stay one more year which she did.

Two years had passed now and Belize was entering high school, getting more beautiful everyday. Rudy was really keeping an eye on her even more now. Maryann called everyday. Granny and Ms. Irene had an annual Saturday girls day to go shopping.

It was the end of the school year and Belize's team had won the state championship in basketball with Belize being the most valuable player, so they were out celebrating, Also Belize would be going home in two days which she didn't want to but knew she had to. The two days went by fast Belize said her goodbyes and she was headed back to the south.

★★★★★

Granny and Ms. Irene was coming from the airport dropping off Belize headed out to shop again.

"Let me stop by the house and pick up something Irene before we go anywhere else." Granny headed back to the house. When she got there Unc Pete was sitting on the front porch. He had his head in his hands. Harold was looking around lost. Granny knew something was wrong. She got out the car and walked up to the porch.

"What's wrong with you two old birds sitting here looking like you just lost your best friend?"

"The feds just raided Rudy and Zack's office. They have them in jail again. This time for tax invasion and conspiracy."

"What?"

Ms. Irene got outta the car. She saw the shock look in Granny's face and knew something was wrong.

★★★★★

A thousand miles away in a courtroom in the south in North Carolina stood Rico, smiling. He had just won his appeal and got ten years knocked off his sentence for a technically. He would be coming home soon. Rico didn't know at the same time his cousin was going in jail miles away.

Sitting in the courtroom with her legs crossed watching was Queenie, a red bone curvaceous lady with long silky curly hair. A true knockout and Rico's new wife. They had been married one year now and she was expecting a child. He got congeal visits while he was inside prison after he got married. She was all smiles, a young beautiful girl from the neighborhood who always was amazed by the toughness of Rico. It was a dream come true for her to be his wife and six months pregnant by him. She was there every visit and at home waiting on every call. She worked in the local Kmart as a cashier. As Rico walked out the courtroom back into the back, smiling, she blew him a kiss. He knew it won't be long now.

CHAPTER 13

Sitting at her big wooden desk with the walls lined up with certificates and awards, Maryann looked back out the window that had a good view of the city. She took in a deep breath as the phone ranged.

"Hello may I help you?"

"Maryann this is Granny."

"Hey Granny how you doing?"

"Not too good baby not too good."

"Why, what's wrong?"

"They just raided Rudy's office. Him and Zack are in jail again for tax invasion."

"What? How did that happen. I thought everything was worked out?"

"That's what I thought but it seems these people have it in for them or something."

"Let me make a few calls and I'll call you right back." Maryann called around the federal offices and founded out that Rudy and Zack had been under investigation for the last 8 years. They never stopped watching them, they just didn't wanna arrest them without no solid evidence.

It was reported that money once again was being laundered through their strip club this time and Rudy and Zack were the invisible face behind the biggest heroin operation in California. Maryann couldn't believe it, as she held the phone listening.

She immediately took a leave of absence from work. Driving home she was contemplating how she would tell Belize what was going on with her father. She pulled into the driveway with Belize sitting on the porch writing. Belize looked up and smiled at her mother and walked over to the car.

"Hey Momma."

"Hey baby."

"What's wrong with you?"

"Well I don't know how to say it any other way."

"What?"

"They arrested your father again. He's in jail."

"In jail for what?"

"Tax invasion and conspiracy."

"Momma we gotta go help him he needs us please?"

"Yeah I know. I'm crazy for doing it but that's all I been telling myself riding home. We gotta go help him. So go get packed, we going to California." As Maryann got out the car she couldn't help but think about how things could have been if Rudy would have just stay honest and got out and worked with the government like she did. She also thought about her career and life with Belize. She knew her father was her heart and it would be hard to turn her against her father no matter what he did. Maybe I can convince him to get outta that life if we get back together maybe I can, I still love that man I do, she thought. Walking in the house she felt like the world was on her shoulders. She just sat down on the couch and relaxed as Belize got ready upstairs the phone rang again.

"Yes hello?"

"What happen Maryann?"

"Well they said they been watching them for a while and they think they got them this time."

"Got them for what?"

"Running the biggest heroin operation in California."

"What? Where did all that nonsense come from? I know them boys got a girl dance club but they don't do nothing else."

"I hope and pray so, Granny, I hope and pray so."

"Does Belize know what happen?"

"Yes she's upstairs getting packed."

"Packed for what?"

"We on our way, leaving tonight."

"Thank you so much, You know that man still loves you and Belize is his world. That will mean so much to him y'all being here."

"Yeah I know. I took a leave of absence. I'll call you when we board. Let me start getting packed Granny."

"Okay talk to you later and thank you again." Granny hung up the phone fighting back tears. As Ms. Irene put her arms around her Unc Pete sat on the couch looking lost thinking to himself how did this happen. The next morning Maryann, Belize, Unc Pete, Granny and Ms. Irene were sitting in the federal courtroom waiting on the arraignment for Rudy and Zack. After being there an hour out the boys came in shackles. They sat down by their lawyer and went through the proceedings. The judge ordered no bail and continued their case.

★★★★★

"What does that mean, Momma?"

"It means they ain't gonna let your Daddy out. They gotta go to court in a month."

"Why so long why they making him wait so long?"

"Baby I don't know."

"Momma you work for them can't you do something?"

For the first time Maryann realized she was on the other side but sitting with the enemy. She noticed the looks she was getting from the prosecutor. It would come a time in the near future were Maryann was going to have to choose her career or her family. Rudy looked back at them and smiled he seemed to be okay.

"Hey Daddy I love you," Belize blurted out.

"Young lady you will be removed from the courtroom with another outburst like that."

"We leaving anyway," Belize said sarcastically.

"Belize don't speak to that man like that. That wasn't nice," Maryann responded.

"Well he wasn't nice to my Daddy. I don't care." Belize stormed out the courtroom with everyone looking at her, this was the first time Maryann or anyone had heard her be defiant. Granny and Unc Pete and Ms. Irene got up and they all went out the courtroom.

"I don't know what's wrong with her."

"She seeing how the system works in America that's all," Unc Pete said.

"Well if her Daddy would go by the law he wouldn't have problems."

"The law, what law?"

"I just hope and pray Rudy ain't doing the things they said he is."

"Honey everything will work out. What them boys need now is our prayers and love."

"I don't care what they say about my Daddy. He ain't did nothing wrong to nobody."

Maryann looked at her daughter. She was growing up fast and she prayed she hadn't made a mistake letting Belize come out here for the summers. They all walked out the courtroom to the cars and got in headed for Granny's house. Unc Pete, Ms. Irene, and Granny in one car Maryann and Belize following them. When they got to the house the phone rang soon as they got in the house.

"Hello?"

"Hey Granny how y'all doing?" It was Rudy sounding down a little.

"Baby don't let them people worry you. It's gonna be alright."

"Yeah I know but I just don't understand. Where they getting all this information they say they have?"

"What information baby?"

"The lawyer told us they have an informant who can testify that we have been laundering old drug money and new money through the club."

"What?"

"Yep that's why they holding us and been watching us the whole time because of an informant."

"Well don't worry baby. It will all workout."

"Is Maryann there? I need to speak to her, Granny."

"Yes hold on baby." Granny handed the phone to Maryann.

"Hello?"

"Hey there sweetheart. Please just listen."

"I'm listening."

"I told you I was through with that life and I was and I am. I don't know where all this came from."

"Well I did some checking and they got an informant who has made a sworn statement against y'all and it might be enough to convict you and get everything you own seized. Have you thought about that, what it would do to your daughter?"

"Yes I have and I won't let it happen. I promise you that."

"And you know what's crazy? I was thinking bout you lately, really thinking bout giving you another chance."

"Well don't stop thinking bout us then because y'all all I got baby. I promise things will work out just stick by me. Can you please do that?"

"Yes but don't lie to me again about nothing Rudy you hear me?"

"I won't."

"Let me speak to Daddy." It was Belize in the back ground. "Hey Daddy, hey Daddy."

"Hey there little lady what you doing?"

"Nothing, at Granny's."

"Well you don't worry bout Daddy I will be okay."

"Daddy I'll come and break you out I ain't scared of them police."

"Nah baby don't do that. I gotta get out the right way. Hopefully it won't be too much longer. You be good and you know Daddy loves you and whatever you do, keep making them songs. Don't forget you a star. I got a buddy in Los Angeles that works at a record company. I sent him your music and he has Granny's number. I was going to surprise you but I'm here. Hopefully you will be getting a call from him soon."

"I won't stop and thank you so much Daddy. I know they gonna call and like it. I know they is I love you Daddy." Belize handed the phone to her Mother.

"Listen I'm bout to call the lawyer. We'll be down there Saturday for visiting. They talking bout at least holding you until your next court date, a month from now. I'll see if I can make some calls and get you a bail."

"Thank you baby, Love you."

"Yeah I really hope you do because I'm bout to put my whole life on the line for you."

"I do. Never forget that."

Maryann hung up the phone. "I need to go make some calls to Washington, Granny do you have any leftovers? I'm starving."

"Me too."

"Yeah I could use something to eat also," Ms. Irene said.

"What bout you Unc Pete? You hungry too?"

"Nah I'm okay. I need to make some runs," Unc Pete said headed out the door. He had one thing on his mind, he was going to find out who the snitch was in the circle. He couldn't believe one of his buddies would turn on him for what they had no reason to. Unc Pete got in his car and drove off after driving for a while he pulled into a parking lot and went to the pay phone and went into the booth inserting the coins in.

"Hello? Yeah this Pete."

"Hey what's up buddy?"

"Listen I got some funny shit going on up here. I need you to check the backgrounds of some people around me. I hope it don't come back crazy."

"Well give me their names and I'll have you the answers tonight."

Unc Pete gave the listener the names of his associates he was working with.

"Listen also checkout everyone in the families I'm around for any kind of current cases pending or any red flags employment anything."

"I got you. Call me later on."

"Listen I'll just hit you in the morning."

"That's fine with me."

★★★★★

Back at the courthouse in the holding cell sat Rudy and Zack.

"Man this shit is crazy. What the fuck are they talking bout?"

"I don't know. We good. Don't trip."

"We got an enemy somewhere that wants us locked up." That shit turned a light on in Rudy's head. Enemy — who else could it be but that punk azz police chief who been following them around.

"It got to be the police chief."

"Well don't worry we covered on all ends so we just gotta play their waiting game that's all buddy."

"Yeah but fuck Zack I never saw this coming. We were out."

"And we still out."

★★★★★

Maryann was in the other room speaking to her superiors in Washington she was holding the phone with a shocked look on her face. They had just told her she was also being investigated and her leave had just been turned into a suspension until further notice.

"I worked hard for you and this is the thanks I get?"

"I'm sorry. There's nothing I can do. The orders came down."

"Well to hell with you and whoever sent them." She hung up the phone crying, Belize came into the room.

"Momma what's wrong?"

"I don't have a job. Them people think I have something to do with whatever they think your father did."

"Well you ain't did nothing, or Daddy, so don't worry Momma everything will be okay, Don't cry Momma." Belize put her arm around her mother as Granny walked in the room over hearing the conversation.

"Listen Maryann this family will make it through this. Yes we will. Worrying ain't gonna help. Y'all come on in here and get something to eat."

"Okay here we come. Belize let's go wash ours hands."

Belize and Maryann walked up the stairs to the bathroom passing by the guest room. There was someone in there. Belize peeped in, it was Mr. Harold on the phone. She walked closer to him.

"I've given you as much as I can. I don't know nothing else on them," Harold said.

"Well you better find something nigger or your azz is going to jail with them and your fucking son will rot in that prison. You will never see him free do you hear me?"

"Yes I hear you. I will keep trying."

Harold's son was in prison in South Carolina for murder. This all happen before he met Ms. Irene and she knew nothing of this.

The chief of police during his investigation discovered the love Harold had for his son and knew he was the weak link to break the chain to get to Rudy and Zack so he contacted Harold and told him get him some solid evidence on the boys and he would get his son home. So the whole time Harold was around he was trying to come up with something. That's why he was always so quiet but Rudy, Zack, and Unc Pete never let him near them at all when they were talking any business it was all done inside the fort at the garage.

"Were you talking bout my father? Who were you talking to?" Belize said.

"Hey don't be sneaking up on me like that," Harold said scared to death.

"Who were you talking to bout my father?"

"What are you talking bout young lady? I think you misunderstood what you heard. That was grown folks talk."

Belize stared at him hard then walked out the door and ran down to the kitchen were Granny was and told Granny what had happen. She just stood there for a moment.

"Don't you mention this to no one, not even your mother, you hear me."

"Yes, ma'am."

"Hand me the phone." Granny dialed Unc Pete's number.

"Pete, come over here ASAP. It's important."

"What's wrong?"

"You need to get over here immediately." Granny hung up the phone and Unc Pete stared at the receiver for a moment. He jumped up and headed straight to Granny's house. He was there in what seemed like minutes. He walked in the door. Everyone was at the table eating including Harold.

Pete spoke to everyone. "Hey Granny I really need to speak to you for a moment. Could I have a minute please?"

Granny got up and walked with Unc Pete to the back room. Belize looked over at Harold. She knew what Unc Pete was there for. Harold expression never changed, he continued to eat his food.

Granny sat Unc Pete down and told him what Belize had told him. Unc Pete got redder and redder clenched his fist with every word. "So that why they keep fucking with us? That muthafucka but why?"

"I don't know, Pete, I don't know. Jealously maybe."

"No it got to be more than that."

"Well I know he low down dirty bastard for what he doing."

"Yeah don't worry bout him. I'll take care of that tomorrow. I'm waiting on a call now. Matter of fact let me use your phone." Unc Pete called his buddy back and added Harold's name to the list. He hung up the phone and walked back into the kitchen. Everyone was finishing up the meal.

"Well I gotta go right quick. I will see you all tomorrow." Unc Pete walked out the door fuming. He wanted to kill Harold sitting there. All he wanted to know now was why.

The next morning he was awoken by a phone call and he got the answer. His buddy told him all about Harold's son and that's was enough reason for Pete to believe he was trying to set the family up. That next evening, late night, Unc Pete went over to Ms. Irene's house and crept into their driveway unseen. He crawled under Harold's car and ran a wire from his starter to his gas tank. Unc Pete went back to the house and went to sleep anticipating the news the next morning he knew he would hear.

"Pete! Pete! Wake up, wake up."

"Granny what's wrong?"

"Someone killed Irene and Harold their car blew up in their driveway this morning." Granny had a feeling that Pete knew who had did it.

"What? How did that happen?"

"He was dropping her off this morning to work. Her car wasn't working."

"Damn." Pete could hear chaos in the background.

"All this is getting outta control Pete."

"I'm on my way." Pete sat in bed thinking at least the snitch was gone he didn't mean to kill Irene too but what could he do now bout it? She was gone.

★★★★★

Maryann walked in the living room as Granny was hanging up the phone.

"Lord have mercy on this family. I don't know what I've got me and my baby involved in."

"The papers trying to make it more than it is Maryann."

"Yeah cause it's a big headline right here that says 'Mob hit suspected as explosion kills two people'."

Granny closed her eyes and begins to cry. Maryann looked back as Belize stood in the doorway, listening, thinking of her father.

CHAPTER 14

The music melody was soft and warm and departed was the theme that played from the piano as the few people in all black sat in the rows of benches and mourned the loss of a love one. The building was old but well—kept with pictures of Jesus Christ hanging from the rafters, large windows that were stained provided the light of the day shining through. This was one of the few local black Baptist churches in town, the one that Granny had become a member of and there she sat in tears in the front row hunched over unable to stop shaking and crying. Maryann sat beside Granny with Belize on the other side. Annie and Zack's father were sitting next to her.

"Lord Lord Lord why did this have to happen? Lord Lord."

"Granny she at peace now. She's in a better place than we are."

"She didn't deserve to die like that though."

"I know, I know she didn't. She was a good woman."

"Lord Lord Lord please."

Belize held on tight to her Granny as she also cried with her. She loved Ms. Irene also dearly.

"Granny, Granny, don't cry, don't cry."

"Baby, baby, she's gone. Irene is gone." Granny started shaking really hard and jerking. Maryann tried to hold her as she jerked away from her. Belize was pushed down to the floor. Granny went into a shock and fell on the floor beside Belize with her eyes in the back of her head and still shaking. She was in shock or having a seizure.

"Call for help! Call for help! I think Granny is dying. Pastor, someone, hurry and call for help! call for help," said Maryann straddling Granny as she began rubbing her head and feeling for her pulse.

"Granny, Granny, Granny, wake up. Wake up."

"Momma, what's wrong with Granny? What's wrong with Granny, Momma?"

"Baby, I don't know. I don't know."

Belize ran to the back. As she did the preacher man came out. "They're on their way. The ambulance is on its way."

"When? When they say they coming?"

"Now they coming, now."

Belize went back over to Granny no longer shaking now barely breathing. "Granny, hold on, Granny. The ambulance is coming, hold on."

"Prop her head up with my coat. Put it under her," said Zack's father.

In the background you could hear the sirens coming. The organ music had come to a halt. The paramedics rushed in and put Granny on a stretcher and loaded her into the ambulance. Maryann and Belize rode with her. Within minutes they were there. Sitting in the emergency room waiting for what seemed like hours. Finally out comes the doctors as Annie's and Zack's father walks in the door.

"How is Granny?"

"There's the doctor right there," Maryann said getting up and pointing walking in the doctor's direction at the same time.

"So how's she doing, Doctor?"

"She's holding on. We have her in the intensive care."

"Intensive care? What you mean? What's wrong with her?" Belize said.

"Your Grandmother had a stroke. She's a strong woman, hopefully she will come around."

"What do you mean hopefully?"

"Right now, we don't know."

"Grannyyyy!" Belize screamed and ran into the back rooms where she thought Granny was.

"Hey ma'am you can't go back there." The doctor turned and tried to stop her but it was too late.

Standing at Granny beside with tears in her eyes was Belize.

"Granny, please, Granny wake up. Don't die please, Granny. I need you, Granny. Daddy needs you. We got too much to do. Please wake up Granny."

Maryann walked in with tears in her eyes and put her arms around her daughter as Annie and Zack's father came into the room with the doctor.

"Listen I understand how you feel but right now the best thing for her is rest and attention from us. We can't have you people in here. You are more than welcomed to wait in the lobby.

"Come on baby. She's sleep right now. We'll wait in the lobby. She will be okay. She will be okay."

"Momma. Momma, Granny got to wake up. She got to wake up."

They all walked out of the room. Belize walked back over and kissed Granny on the cheek.

"I love you, Granny." Then she walked out of the room and joined the others in the lobby as Unc Pete walked through the door.

"Unc Pete, Granny ain't breathing. She had a stroke. She had a stroke."

"My God how does she look?"

"She's not conscience right now. The doctors said hopefully with rest she will come out of it."

Unc Pete sat down and put his head in his hands. He couldn't believe how fast things were hitting this family but he also understood what happens in war. How would Rudy take this, was what was on his mind.

★★★★★

In the TV room in the quad of the cells at federal holding sat Rudy and Zack watching the news. It was showing footage of the car bombing in the city that killed a local couple. Rudy and Zack turned instantly to each other with blank stares on their face.

"What the fuck is going on?" Zack said.

"I don't know but we need to find out." Rudy jumped up and called the house over and over getting no answer. He called all the numbers he knew. He couldn't reach no one.

"Something is going on I can't reach no one."

"No one?"

"Man what the fuck?"

"Say buddy can I use the phone? You been standing there just holding it. I need to call my people."

"Not right now, we busy." Zack looked at the inmate.

"Fuck that. I need to use the phone."

"Here you go," Rudy said as he smashed the phone into the inmates face and head until he hit the ground. After that Rudy began stomping him.

"Rudy! He through. He's through, Rudy." Zack grabbed his friend before he caught another charge in there.

"I guess next time you'll wait muthafucka," Zack said as he kicked the inmate on the ground.

"Man what the fuck is going on?"

"I don't know but we don't need no murders in here."

"Yeah yeah."

Zack could see the rage in Rudy's eyes.

"Call the lawyer. Call the lawyer." After a few rings the lawyer receptionist answered the phone. She put Rudy through.

"Hello Rudy how you doing?"

Rudy could hear something in the voice of the lawyer. "I'm cool. What's going on?"

"Well I have some bad news for you."

"Give it to me. What happen?"

"Granny had a stroke at Ms. Irene's funeral. She's in intensive care."

"What? What did you say? How? What the fuck?" Rudy slammed the phone receiver against the wall.

"What's wrong?" Zack asked as Rudy held the receiver not saying nothing.

"Granny had a stroke at Ms. Irene's funeral. She's in the hospital."

"Oh shit what the fuck? Is she okay?"

"He said she's in intensive care."

"That's why no one was answering the phones huh?"

"Yeah."

"Rudy?"

"Yeah and they ain't the start of it."

"Yeah what else."

"They going for the Rico Act against you boys. They got it all in the papers. Also with that car bomb, they trying to tie this into the underworld. They looking at Unc Pete hard. I'm going to talk to him right now. I was going to stop down at the jail afterward and see you guys."

"What time man? You gotta get us the fuck outta here."

"You gotta play the waiting game. It's nothing you or I can do. With no bail, no money can spring you."

"Well get us a fucking bail then."

"I'm doing everything I can. Y'all pissed someone off. They really want your heads Rudy."

"Fuck them. I want their heads too. I'm tired of this shit, them fucking with us."

"Listen, I got a funny phone call from the feds not too long ago. An agent that said he was willing to help y'all. Je said he knew you from the military, knew you were good guys. That's what I wanna talk to you about."

"What? Who you talking about?"

"I don't know. He wouldn't leave his name we suppose to meet next week though but he said he was in the military with both of you."

"I don't know right now. Listen this is what I need you to do I need you to go to that hospital and get a number from them that I can call collect to. I need to speak to Granny."

"She's unconscious right now, Rudy. You can't speak to her."

"Well get a fucking number where I can speak to Maryann. What the fuck man?"

"Okay calm down, calm down. I know you upset."

"Calm down, my azz. Get over there why you still on the phone."

"Rudy what did he say?"

Rudy told Zack everything then sat down and closed his eyes. He never imagined the day when he would be without Granny in life. Losing Maryann was enough. He couldn't lose Granny. He bowed his head and prayed and asked God to watch over her and forgive him for what he had did and please don't take it out on his family.

"I wonder who he talking bout say they know us from the military?"

"I don't know or give a fuck right now." Rudy went into his cell and laid down. Zack grabbed the phone and began making calls.

★★★★★

Back at the hospital in emergency sat everyone. Belize was sleep on Maryann shoulder, Annie and Zack's father were sitting there, not really saying too much. They were acting strange but with all the chaos, Maryann played it no mind.

"Maryann I know this might not be a good time but..."

"But what? What's wrong now?"

"Well we leaving. We can't take it out here no more. It's too fast and dangerous for us. We going back to the south. We have enough saved to get us a good home and live comfortably."

"What about, Zack?"

"Zack is a big boy. He will be okay. Plus he got old Pete over there to watch over him."

"Imah miss you. It was nice having you around."

"I know. I'm miss all of y'all but this place is just too much," Annie said as she walked over and hugged Maryann and Unc Pete. She didn't really know everything that was going on but she had a feeling it was about to get worse. She knew it was best for her to take her sober husband back to the country. She had been waiting for him to get sober all these years and just live a quiet life.

"Hopefully Zack will call the house before you leave."

"Well if not we'll get in contact with him when we get there. Our planes leaves in two hours."

"What y'all wasn't playing?"

"No Maryann I'm serious. I don't like living here no more never really did to be honest with you."

"I do understand Annie I love and will miss you." Maryann got up and hugged her. Belize was slouched over in the chair still sleep.

"Well Pete we'll call you all when we get there. Good—bye and we pray Granny will be alright," Annie said as she grabbed Zack father's hand and they walked out the doors headed for their car and to the airport having already planned this before they even went to the funeral.

★★★★★

Two and a half months had passed and Granny hadn't gotten no better coming in and outta consciousness but never regaining it fully. One morning laying in his cell nodding off Rudy is awaken by the guards.

"You have a visitor. Your lawyer wants to talk to you."

Zack was standing by the door outside the cell that lead to the visiting room Rudy got up groggy, wiped his face, straighten out his clothes a little, and walked in the sally port. The last few months had been rough on Rudy, mentally. He was an angry person. He wanted to kill something, everyone who had caused this pain to come into his family.

"What's up Zack? The lawyer huh?"

"Yeah shit. I hope he has a court date for us soon, to spring us outta here."

"I hope so too."

The boys walked outta the cell block down the hall into the interviewing room and sat at the table were the lawyer was waiting for them at, with a strange look on his face.

"How you doing Rudy? How you doing Zack?"

"I'm cool what's up?"

"How you doing, sir?" Zack responded.

"I don't know any other way to say this Rudy."

"Say what?" Rudy stood up.

"Granny died early this morning in her sleep, Rudy."

"Oh my God." Rudy crumbled to the floor crying and sobbing uncontrollably as Zack stood there in shock.

"Man this is fucked up. Man this is fucked up." Zack knelt down and hugged his friend as they both sat on the floor crying like babies.

"Hey, y'all gotta get up off that floor," the guard said opening the door peeking in.

"Their Grandmother just died. Be light on them, Deputy."

He looked at the lawyer and then at Rudy and Zack who never even looked up at the deputy.

"Just make it fast," he said as he shut the door.

Rudy and Zack got back up. The lawyer didn't really know what to say for a moment.

"Well maybe this will be some good news to you. That federal agent says he can get the case to disappear for a fee fellas."

"What did you say?"

"We can beat this case is what I said fellas."

"So did you ever meet with this dude and find out who he was for real?"

"I did find out he was stationed in Thailand with you guys. You all were discharged around the same time. His family is from Kentucky does that ring a bell?"

Both of them looked at each other Rudy still with tears coming down his face.

"When can you get us outta here? I need to be with my daughter and wife."

"I can have y'all back in court in a few weeks at the latest but you will walk when you go this time with the help of your friend."

"What will it take to get us out for my Granny's funeral?"

"I'm sorry Rudy but that ain't gonna happen. The feds don't allow that at all."

"What the fuck kinda shit is that?"

"I guess this the payback huh?" Rudy put his head down and tears began to come out again. Zack put his arm around his friend after a few minutes the guard put his head in the door.

"Okay gentlemen your time is up."

"Listen Rudy, Maryann and I will handle everything. Your Granny will be sent off in class. I promise you that."

"Thank you, very much, thank you."

"Yeah thanks, man," Zack said to him as they both got up and walked outta the room.

For days Rudy was just in his cell quiet. Zack was getting worried about him.

After Granny funeral had passed Maryann and Belize ran the restaurant and came to the jail as much as they could. Belize went in a writing mode staying in her room when she was home with the earphones on and pen and pad. Even when she was in the car riding all she did was write. Maryann realized it was her way of mourning.

★★★★★

Outside the state prison in North Carolina a month and a half later stood Queenie by her car on some pretty brown legs sticking out of a tight dress that showed off her curvaceous figure. Her hair was hanging from her shoulders blowing in the wind. Her legs were shaking as she patted her feet up and down on the ground waiting for those big massive doors to open. She had been there two hours waiting with her newborn baby girl, Coco in a basket in the back seat of the car, eyes wide open sucking on her bottle waiting for her poppa she had never seen. Rico was finally coming home. The man Queenie had been waiting for her whole life.

A loud horn sounded off as the fences began to slide open one after another one as she looked. There he was standing there behind the last one. Finally eyes connecting with each other, Rico walked to his freedom and into the arms of his wife. He was finally a free man again. No parole, nothing. A clean state outta there, time served, with the time he had in and the time cut he got from the appeal.

The closer Rico got to Queenie the faster his pace got. She bounced in her shoes smiling at him as he got to her. He wrapped his arms around her and lifted her from the ground.

"Hey baby. Damn you feel good in my arms."

"So do you," Queenie said as she laid a wet kissed on his lips and he slid his tongue into her mouth smoothly and slowly. They stood there for a moment as the fences began to close behind them.

"Hey looked in the back seat. It's a pretty lady that's been waiting here with me."

"Ohh my goodness there she go. There's my little angel." Rico open the car door and took Coco out of the basket and held his baby girl close to him for the first time in the free world.

"Damn baby this feels so good. This is what I been waiting on for so long."

"Well you don't have to wait no more."

"Yeah let's get the fuck outta here. I don't wanna see this shit for another second of my life," Rico said as he got into the front seat with Coco in his arms.

"That sound good to me baby." Queenie walked around and got into the car and started the engine as they pulled out to a free life.

"So we still moving to California Rico?"

"Hell yeah. I'm going to get my money from Auntie ASAP. Plus my little cousin out there rolling, so we good."

"Your momma told me not to tell you while you were in there but your Auntie in California had a stroke. She died like a month ago.

"What Rudy's Momma?"

"Yep she died."

"Damn we gotta go. We leaving in the morning baby."

"Good cause I'm ready. I was hoping you didn't wanna hang around here to long."

"Nah baby we done seen enough of the country. Momma can stay here if she want to but we out. Ain't that right Coco?" Rico held his daughter up bouncing her as the baby smiled and made facing at him.

"California here we come baby."

CHAPTER 15

Two weeks later in the back of an empty courtroom, sat three gentlemen – two in suits and white shirts obviously. The fed next to them wearing wore out jeans and construction boots with a tight jean jacket on with some iron rim glasses sitting on his nose and a smear expression on his face sat an elderly white man who seemed to mad at the world for some reason.

Belize, she sat still, several rows up, staring directly at the older Whiteman behind the big wooden desk with the black robe on. Maryann sat beside her holding her hand. Unc Pete was next to her.

Rudy and Zack were sitting with their lawyer, leaned forward in their chairs anticipating the moment they had been waiting for.

Finally after the judge had studied all the paperwork before him, he announced, "I find that this case will be dismissed due to a lack of evidence. The defendants are now free to go," he said without a smile on his face as he slammed the mallet down.

"Alright alright! That's what I'm talking bout. Justice." Belize jumped up and ran to hug her dad as he walked towards her and to his freedom. Zack was smiling as he shook the lawyer's hand.

"That solider boy came through for y'all."

"Yeah well he owe us that."

179

"I would advise you guys to disappear for a while."

"Good advice. We'll take it too. Thanks again."

Unc Pete walked up to Zack and hugged him.

"What in the hell kinda law is this? What is this? These are murders and drug dealers! Murders and drug dealers!"

Maryann looked back and it was the elderly white man she had noticed was looking very strange behind them the whole time screaming out loud.

"Order in the court! Order in the court," the judge yelled as he slammed his mallet down. The two federal agent were holding back the old man as he was trying to reach the area were Rudy and Zack were at.

"Them muthafuckers didn't have shit on y'all. It was just a waiting game, that's all," said Unc Pete.

"Yeah well I'm tired of their games. Ay where mom and dad at?"

"They left, son. They went back home."

"What?"

"They left. They said they couldn't take it no more."

"The big city ain't for everybody. Maybe it was for the best," responded Zack.

"It ain't over you niggers and nigger lovers. It ain't over!"

"Who is that?" said Unc Pete.

"Oh that's an old buddy of me and Rudy's." Zack put his arms around Unc Pete as they followed everyone out the doors of the courtroom to the doors of the street. They got into the cars and pulled off headed once again to Granny's house. This time she wasn't gonna be there though as Rudy rode with Maryann with Belize in the car.

180

"So what are your plans now, Mr. Rudy?" Maryann said driving looking straight ahead with Belize leaning up listening.

"I'm just wanna have my family back and take care of them. That's all."

"Zack's mother and father left. They couldn't take it anymore. I don't know if I can either."

"All I ever wanted to do was make you and my baby happy. That was all."

"I don't know. I don't know, Rudy. This is driving me crazy, all this."

"We run a legit business and you know that."

"No. I don't know nothing."

"You do know you still love me and I still love you and we love our angel back there and we need to be together as a family. You do know that deep inside don't you?"

"My career is probably over cause of this."

"Why you say that?"

"Long story."

"Baby, all I know is we gonna be alright if we together. I can't lose you. Granny gone. Y'all all I have."

"Momma, we gotta stay. We belong with daddy. He needs us."

"Well what do I have to lose? What do I have to lose?"

"Nothing. Only the world to gain baby."

They all sat in silence and continued riding towards Granny's house with Unc Pete and Zack following them.

"Oh yeah your cousin Rico has been calling you."

"Rico from down south?"

"Yes that Rico."

"What he say?"

"He's out of prison and has moved to California. He's living in Vallejo. He's married and has a daughter and has a job in Humbo County somewhere. I told him you were going to court today hopefully coming home." Rudy got quiet for a moment thinking about how his whole life had changed since he meet Rico.

"You alright?"

"Yep I'm okay. And we gonna be alright, baby, we gonna be alright. I promise you that." He leaned over and kissed Maryann on the cheek and reached back and kissed Belize on the forehead. "Ain't that right superstar?"

"That's right, Daddy."

★★★★★

When they got home that night was magical it seemed, as Maryann and Rudy held each other in their arms in bed for the first time in a long time, going to sleep cheek to cheek, waking up, making love over and over.

Days past and finally Rico called and caught up with Rudy.

"Hello?"

"May I speak to Rudy?"

"Daddy, telephone."

"Is this my little cousin who I been hearing so much about?"

"Who is this?"

"This is your cousin Rico."

"Hi."

"How you doing?"

"I'm okay."

"You know I have a baby girl. Imah bring her down there so you can see your little cousin."

"Okay. Here's my daddy."

"Hello?"

"Rudy, Rudy, Rudy."

"What's up Rico Boy?"

"Cousin thanks for looking out for me and I'm sorry to hear about Auntie."

"Yeah. We just taking it easy round here one day at a time. Granny is missed every moment of everyday."

"So listen I need to come see you."

"Well when you coming?"

"I'll be down there this weekend."

"Okay call me when you get ready to hit the highway."

"Cuz thanks again."

"It was nothing. It was nothing. We family, never forget that. I really need you to settle down and stay home."

"I'm home folks. I ain't going nowhere."

"See you this weekend."

"Love you Cuz."

"Love you too Rico."

Maryann stood back and looked at the man she couldn't deny and put her arms around her daughter and closed her eyes.

★★★★★

In an office across town on the twelfth floor behind some closed doors and Venetian blinds stood three men ranting and raving.

"I don't know how the fuck it happen!"

"Somebody on our side is playing with them."

"It gotta be."

"What the fuck else could it be? That fucking car was blew up on purpose then all of a sudden the evidence gets dropped."

"That wasn't the main reason. The prosecutor claimed he said the paperwork was all correct and all weapons found were registered to them."

"I don't care. I don't give a fuck. They guilty and I'm see to it they go to jail or die in the streets."

"Now, wait a minute."

The chief of police walked outta the feds office with one thought on his mind − killing Rudy and Zack. All he had to do was find them.

★★★★★

Two days later early in the morning sitting at the kitchen table overlooking eggs, grits, bacon and fresh toast with a glass of orange juice beside each plate loving every minute of this life was Rudy.

"Good morning, Daddy. Good morning, Momma."

"Hey Princess."

"Good morning, Belize. You just getting up?"

"I was writing all night trying to finish up a few things."

"One day all that hard work gonna pay off baby girl. Watch what I tell you."

"I know, Daddy, I know. That's why I don't and won't stop."

"We going to Hollywood, yes we is."

"Y'all better not forget me. I know that."

"Momma we a team till the end. you know that."

"You better know it. Now sit down and let's eat baby."

They all started laughing and sat and ate the good food Maryann had made. She was a terrific cook, something Rudy loved about her.

"So what do you have planned for this morning?"

"I'm going out and looking at some properties that we need to invest in."

"Well I'm going to get alotta records transferred then I gotta go to that bank and then see if these people are going to give me my same salary."

"Momma they got to. You know how to do the job."

"I was lucky to get my job back and get transferred."

"Listen I know I've took you guys through a lot. Thank you, both of you, for not giving up on me and loving me."

"Daddy, we a team till the end. Right, Momma?"

"That's right."

"Well we bout to go into the real estate business. Imah sell Zack my interest in the clubs and stay completely away from that lifestyle."

"Thank GOD."

"So Unc Zack still gonna keep the clubs?" Belize knew she could get her music played there and she liked the atmosphere anyway.

"Yep he's says he's gonna keep them open. We weren't doing nothing wrong."

"Well I'm glad you saw the light. Don't no married man need to be around naked women all day. No way." Maryann said as she got up grabbing everyone's plate.

"You the only naked woman I wanna see the rest of my life."

"Hey, hey, it's too early in the morning for all that."

"Shoot I'm in love it ain't never too early."

"Yes it is."

"I'm glad you feel that way young lady. You keep thinking like that."

"I don't be thinking bout no boys. I want my career and family that's all." Belize walked out the kitchen into her room as her parents embraced again and held each other tightly.

"Baby the time is coming fast when she will find love."

"Yeah I just hope it's longer than sooner."

The phone rings. After two rings Rudy answers it.

"Hello?"

"Yes my I speak to Belize please?" said a strong male voice on the other end.

"Belize? May I ask who's calling? This is her father."

"Hello good morning, sir. My name is Miles. I'm from Warner Bros records. I work in the A&R department. Your daughter's music got on my desk the other day and I was asked to listen to it."

"Yes." Rudy listened attentively as Maryann walked into the bedroom.

"Well I did and I must say I'm very impressed. I think she has what it takes. I would like for you guys to come to Los Angeles next week so we can sit down and discuss how we can go into business together."

"That, that sounds great."

"Well listen let me give you my contact info. You figure out what day you guys are flying in so I can arrange the rooms and we go from there." Miles gave all his info to Rudy as he wrote it down.

"Hey, thanks Miles for believing in my baby, for real."

"Thank you for bringing her to this world. We bout to make alotta money."

"Sounds good. I'll give you a call next week. Have a good evening."

"You too. Tell Belize we looking forward to meeting her."

"I will. Good—bye."

"Good—bye."

"Belize come mere, baby, come mere!" Rudy was yelling as he hung up the phone.

"What's wrong? What's wrong?" Maryann said coming out of the bedroom.

"What's up daddy?"

"Y'all come mere. Come mere right quick. I told you we was going to Hollywood."

"What happen?"

"I just got off the phone with the A&R department of Warner Brothers Records. They wanna see you in their office next week to see how we can go in business together."

With every word that came outta Rudy's mouth, Belize realized her dream was coming true. She got more excited by the moment and so did Maryann. Her face lit up.

"Oh my God! Oh my God! Daddy, Daddy, you did it! You did it."

"He did what? What did you do, Rudy?"

"I have a friend that works in the music business in Los Angeles and I sent him copies of Belize music to get in the right hands down there a few months ago and we get this call. How bout that, baby, how bout that?"

"Well that's what I'm talking bout. My baby a star."

Rudy got on the phone and called his people in Los Angeles and thanked them. Everything was going so good. The family celebrated all day bumping Belize music over and over dancing and partying as the hours passed in the day.

"Well listen I need to go talk to Zack and Unc Pete. I'll be back later on okay?"

"See you later, Daddy."

"Bye, baby." Maryann walked up and kissed Rudy as he walked out the door connecting to the garage.

"Love you."

"Love you, too." Maryann got against him and felted his gun.

"What's that for?"

"Baby, it's still dangerous out here."

"Just be careful okay."

"I will, baby. I won't be long, okay?"

"Okay." Maryann kissed him again as he closed the door. Rudy walked into the garage, got in his car, slid his gun under the seat, turned the radio on, started the car, and hit the button to open the garage door. He pulled out into the driveway and into the street heading for Unc Pete's. As he drove thru the city with his eyes in the rearview mirror he thought finally he would be able to have some peace in his life. Rudy turned the corner headed into Unc Pete neighborhood a maze of brick homes with well-kept lawns. Rudy went down a ways then made a few more turns and pulled in behind Zack truck, got out and walked to the front door and ranged the doorbell.

"Who is it?"

"It's Rudy."

"Hold on, here I come." The door open in moments.

"How you doing, Rudy?" said Unc Pete.

"I'm okay. Glad all that madness is over."

"I knew they couldn't pen nothing on y'all. It was a waiting game."

"Yeah, well, I'm bout to sell me some houses. Fuck them," Rudy said as he walked into the house. Zack was sitting on the couch watching drag racing.

"What's up, Rudy?"

"Taking it easy, buddy."

"Yeah so listen. I spoke with the lawyer and he gonna handle everything but if you ever want back in the door it will always be open for you."

"Hah I'm cool. I had enough. Imah take the money and run. When will the check be ready?"

"He said he could have everything straighten out by next week."

"Cool."

"So you going to real estate school to get a license huh?" said Unc Pete.

"Oh no. I'm just buy land and build on it or get foreclosure buildings and houses."

"You a smart man. Rudy."

"My instincts telling me to do this and things will workout."

"How's everyone doing?"

"Man they just called from Los Angeles. Some record people I connected Belize with and they like her music. We going down there next week."

"Say what? Well I be damn."

"That little girl was born for the camera, Rudy."

"Yeah she's been through a lot and she kept working hard on her music the whole time. I just gotta make sure this thing don't get outta hand."

"Yeah Hollywood is full of crooks and devils."

"The whole world is."

"You know they ain't gonna stop trying to pen something on us neither."

"We ain't doing shit."

"We got all the paperwork right this time so fuck them, Rudy. I ain't closing my club."

"I'm just tired of the headaches, buddy."

"Shit I'm retired at the garage."

"Y'all know I'm here for you whenever you need me. I just wanna spend more time with Belize and Maryann." Rudy got up and walked towards the door.

"You leaving already?"

"I gotta make a few more stops then head back to the house."

"I'll call you later, buddy."

"Goodnight, Rudy."

"Take it easy Unc Pete." Rudy walked out the door and got into his car pulled off then stopped at the market for some juice. Then he went by the bank and drove on to the house.

The days passed fast. The next week the family was driving down Melrose Boulevard in Los Angeles, looking for a parking garage. They had found the address they were looking for to meet Miles. After parking Rudy, Belize and Maryann walked out into the world of expensive name brand stores and luxury cars they both lined the streets. The smell of money was in the air. Rudy opened the door to the building they were looking for and they walked in and meet the receptionist.

"Yes good morning. May I help you?"

"Yes ma'am. We have an appointment with Miles of Warner Brothers Records."

"And your name sir?"

"Rudy."

The lady picked up the phone looking down at her desk. Belize eased up beside her father as Maryann admired the design of the lobby.

"Yes, sir, go right up to the tenth floor. He's expecting you."

"Thank you."

They walked towards the elevator and entered the elevator. As it lifted them up Belize took a deep breath.

"You okay honey?"

"Yeah Momma, just a little nervous."

"Well you ain't got nothing to worry bout. You a star. They knew it and so do we."

"Just be yourself. We here with you baby."

"I just want to make y'all proud of me, that's all."

"We are very very proud."

"Come mere baby." Rudy hugged his daughter as the doors of the elevator opened to a large sign saying Warner Brothers Records. Standing there was a slim black man with glasses on in a suit.

"Good morning and welcome to LA."

"How you doing, Miles?"

"And this must be Belize."

"Hello. How you doing?"

"I'm doing pretty good. I must say you are a very talented young lady."

"Thank you."

"Well let's go into my office and talk." They follow Miles down the hall into his office. "Would you like something to drink some coffee or juice?

"No, thank you," they all said in unison, laughing, breaking the ice of the moment.

Belize looked around at the gold and platinum records on the wall. Within minutes they were laughing and smiling and negotiating a contract for

Belize. Miles was going to fax the agreement to Rudy's lawyer as soon as they got back. Also Miles had set up a promotional party for Belize in Oakland upon signing the agreement in two weeks. The family walked out smiling.

"Listen when are you guys leaving?"

"We were catching the morning flight."

"Well maybe later on we can go out and grab something to eat and let me show you around the city."

"That would be okay. Is like 7 o'clock alright with you?" Rudy responded.

"Sound good to me," Miles said. That night Miles took them all around LA. They had a ball.

The next morning on the flight home Belize couldn't stop talking bout how her name would be all over the city soon in lights. Deep inside Maryann was scared for her daughter. She had heard the stories of what it would do to people. When they got home and settled in, Rudy and Maryann sat on the couch watching TV.

"Rudy, no matter what, don't let them people turn my daughter into something she's not."

"Don't worry, baby, I got it."

"Yeah but parents always think they in control."

"Listen we raised her well. She has a good idea of what to do."

"She's only a teenager, Rudy."

"Yeah but look who her momma is."

"Flattery will get you nowhere."

"No seriously. I did alotta investigating on their company and this dude Miles."

"So what did they come up with?"

"Well all record companies are shady but this seems to be a decent one for the most part. We just have to stay on the lawyer and make sure Belize is protected."

"Well what has the lawyer been saying?"

"He said Miles is a good dude in the business but understand Belize is a product to them is all he keeps saying."

It was a loud knock at the door then the doorbell rang.

"Who can that be at our door this late? No one comes over here this late." Rudy reached under the couch and got his pistol as he walked up to the door.

"Who is it?"

"It's Rico, Cousin, it's Rico."

Rudy looked at Maryann then open the door slowly.

"What's up, Cousin?"

"Rico, damn. I thought you was coming this weekend."

"Well I took off and came right away. I really needed to see you."

Rudy had gave Rico the address the week before standing beside him was the cutest little girl in the world with a woman who looked like her grown version.

"Well, come on in."

"Cousin, this is my wife Queenie and my daughter Coco."

"Well ain't she a cutie pie? Pretty like her mother. How y'all doing. I'm Rudy."

"Hello. I've heard so much about you and this is my baby Coco."

"Hi Coco. Would you like to go see your big cousin, Belize? She's upstairs."

Coco nodded her head yes. Maryann took Coco up stairs with her to Belize room then she return into the living room.

"Queenie, would you like some tea or coffee? I'm sure these two wanna catch up on old times, have a boys talk." Maryann looked at Rudy.

"Thank you, yes. Tea would be nice."

"Would y'all gentlemen like something to drink?"

"No, I'm just fine."

"Rudy what about you?"

"I'm okay, baby."

Maryann and Queenie walked into the kitchen.

"Damn, Cousin that was some hard ass time I did. Feels like a nigger's birthday to be free."

"Yeah I'm glad to see you out here again."

"So what's the plan?"

"Rico, them Feds on us. I'm through. I got your money. Whatever you wanna do that's on you but I'm cool. I'm be here with my family."

"Shit Cousin, you know me. I don't stop. I got a hook up in jail with the cats in Humbo County on the skunk tip. I'm be super rich in six months. I'm sending all the sticky icky back. Straight back to Greensboro feel me?"

"Yeah I feel ya. I knew it wasn't no coincidence that you were living and working in the weed capital of the world. You something else, boy."

"You know it."

"I'll be right back."

"Damn, Cousin y'all living up in here." As Rico looked around the well−furnished luxurious home.

"Actually this was Granny house. We haven't decided on whether to keep it or not," Rudy said walking back in holding a briefcase.

"Here you go, Cousin. It's all there with some interest."

Rico opened the brief case up and couldn't stop smiling. "Oh yeah I forgot to tell you. Do you remember that old sheriff in Buford? That muthafucka was trying hard to stop my release and he been at all my hearings."

"Is that right?"

"Hell yeah. He wants us bad."

"Well fuck him. That shit is done. You do what you want but I'm finished."

Rico got up as Queenie and Belize and Maryann came down the stairs, Coco holding Belize hand.

The little girl was all smiles. Belize stood back and watched her first true fan.

"Come mere Belize and give your big Cousin Rico a hug." Belize walked over to him and hugged him. They all sat down laughed awhile then Rico and his family left, promising to stay in touch.

As Rico car pulled off he didn't noticed a black van following him to the freeway.

★★★★★

"That's the fucking cousin who just got outta jail. Something is going down. I know it. I know it," thought the sheriff sitting behind the wheel. But what is the question. "It's time for that fucka to die. When he least expect it. I'm coming for you, Rudy."

★★★★★

Two weeks passed and it was the night of Belize record release party. Everyone was so excited. They had been ripping and running all day. Even Rico and his family had come back down for the party. Everyone was ready to leave.

"Rudy, what is taking you so long?" Maryann yelled up the stairs.

"I'm coming baby."

"Belize has to be there for her sound check in twenty minutes."

"Well y'all go ahead. I will meet you there."

"Do you know where it is, Daddy?"

"Yeah baby. I know where the place is at."

"Do you want me to wait and ride with you cousin?"

"Nah Rico, I'm cool. Go ahead and get us some good seats up front. I will meet you there."

"What about Zack and Unc Pete?"

"They gonna meet us there. Y'all go ahead. I will be there right behind y'all. I promise."

"I love you, Daddy."

"I love you to baby and I'm so proud of you. You gonna kill'um tonight, I know."

"Sho is. Bye Daddy, see you there."

"Bye. Y'all drive safe. Be right behind y'all."

The family walked out the door and got into their cars and followed each other to the club.

★★★★★

As they made their way to the freeway, a black van passed them headed in the opposite direction.

"I knew that his cousin was going to lead me right to that muthafucka. And look how this nigger is living! Look at this shit," the sheriff said to himself as he pulled into the residential area were the family lived. He pulled over and unlocked his door was about to get out the car when he saw Rudy coming out the front door.

"Well I'll be damn," he said to himself as he eased the car door closed then began creeping up slowly towards Rudy. When he got within 10 feet, Rudy never noticing him, he raised his gun.

"Say nigger, how you doing?"

Rudy spun around quickly. The first thing he noticed was a shiny object in the man's hand, after he recognized who it was. Before Rudy knew it gunfire filled the air. Within seconds, Rudy laid dead, slumped next to his car with his car keys in his hand.

The sheriff walked back in a hurry to his car, got in and drove away smiling as he passed Rudy's body on the ground.

With all the strength he could muster up, Rudy reached into his jacket pocket and pulled out Belize CD and clutched it as he breathed his last breathe.

★★★★★

Across town walking onto the stage was Belize as the DJ scratched in her hit single blaring from the speakers, "My Daddy, My Daddy, My Daddy, My Daddy was a Mobsta. My Daddy, My Daddy, My Daddy, My Daddy was a Mobsta..."

The End

NOTE FROM THE AUTHOR

To every one of you reading this, I cannot thank you enough for being avid supporters of my work. You all allowed me to make once again one of my dreams a reality. Because you gave me the strength to wanna write something great that could describe why I love life and the streets. This is the third of many of my stories to come, I truly appreciate you taking the time to let my world enter yours.

In closing, I would like to say the only way to change is to do things in life that you never have done before. Your association will always determine your destination. Be careful of the company that you keep and never forget, God always listens to a sinner's prayer.

MAY GOD BLESS ALL YOUR ENDEAVORS

ALSO BY FLEETWOOD

BLOODTEST

HIP HOP TRIED 2 KILL ME

Printed Books on Amazon

Ebooks on Amazon, Barnes & Noble,
iBooks, Kobo, and Sony

PEACE TO ALL MY
T.L. HOMEYS
WHO STAY GAMED UP…

Jesse Clyde (now servin 25 to life), Gigolo Joe, Moose, Little Man, Latrice, Trina, (Rest in Peace to my lil Cuzn Toka we truly miss you), Tiny, Shante, Elray, Twoine, Money Ray, Ramone, (the twins), Terry and Larry a.k.a. Dug, Tony Coleman – Proud of what you doing – BIKES 4LIFE ONE FAM, Doc, Bizzy Ben SFC BOXING, the homey Chill, Frank Tha Bank, Psycho D (R.I.P), Lil Jay–MY NUGGA, Duane, Cornell, Moe, My homey from Peru–Shadow, Samantha, Lil Paul, T–Bone, Peanut, Kiesha, Misty, Tricie, LaLa, T–Top, Filipino Charley, Jay {R.I.P}, Cherry, Lady, Alice, Dodi, Mary, Rene, Chris, Charles, Nima, Nicole, Cyco Mike, Case, Wendy, Price, Jerome, Roshaun (who keep telling me keep on writing love u sis), Eugene, Netta, Lisa, Alf, Woody, my Oakland kinfolk Sam, Ken, Roger the Dodger, Ricky Landerth, DeAngelo, Boo, Arthur and (JaRutha R.I.P.).

PLEASE REST N PEACE
ALL MY HOMEYS

ERIC IVAN FRUCTUOSO – UNITED PLAYA –
SAN FRANCISCO, CA
BIG CLIF–CLIFFORD DEON SNEAD – WEST
OAKLAND, CA
MARVIN EASTER – NORTHSIDE,
MINNEAPOLIS, MN
CAPONE – MEMPHIS, TN
TREYMAINE BROWN – FILLMORE, CA
WARREN CRAWFORD – MOUNT ZION, NC
ERIC SLAUGHTER – NORTHSIDE,
MINNEAPOLIS, MN
ABDUL MUHHEMED – GREENSBORO, NC
WALTER "STUFF" LITTLE, JR –
GREENSBORO, NC
LIL BOOTSIE – GREENSBORO, NC
PETE BROWN – GREENSBORO, NC
STEVE HARLEY – GREENSBORO, NC
KENNETH TATE – GREENSBORO, NC
KENNY BAILEY – GREENSBORO, NC
MIKE BARTLEY – GREENSBORO, NC
CASSANDRA SHELTON – GREENSBORO,
NC

RODNEY LEWIS – HUNTERS POINT, CA
NAPPY – HUNTERS POINT, CA
RONDO – PAGE ST, CA
RAMBO – PAGE ST, CA
ARONDO DAVIS – MINNEAPOLIS, MN
REGGIE MILEY – WASHINGTON, DC
CHUCK – HUNTERS POINT, CA
BIG BEN – HUNTERS POINT, CA
HAMP "MONEY BAGS" BANKS, JR. – SAN FRANCISCO, CA
CHAUNCEY BAILEY, JR. – OAKLAND, CA
OTTO BROWN – SAN FRANCISCO, CA

IT'S TRULY A DAMN SHAME BUT I COULD HAVE EASILY FILLED THIS PAGE UP WITH SO MANY NAMES OF VICTIMS OF VIOLENCE IN THE URBAN COMMUNITY. PLEASE LET'S STOP KILLING EACH OTHER HOMEY AND FOR THE ONES NOT ON HERE, I DIDN'T FORGET YOU, AND YOU'LL NEVER BE FORGOTTEN.

MAY GOD BLESS YOUR SOULS

D.i.r.t.y. M.a.c.k.n.

Devine Inspiration Resurrected Through Youth

*Masters of Art Communication
Knowledge and Networking*

Coming Soon

The Dirty Mack'n Trybe

Bang'n 4 Brown

Nenyo Brown (M.I.P.), Ray Ryda,
Dirty Tracks, Lil Ceez,

Big Duke, Dolla Bill, Dirty Ren, Lil Bruh, Swav,

Wes Mack'n, J−Smalls, Big Keith Sinotra, Don Juan,

Graphix by Dirty Ren−thedirtiestren@yahoo.com

Facebook search: Ren Black

Also coming soon
DMT Urban Apparel...

**B.W.B.C. Media - Graphic design, Motion
Graphix, Video Editing and Compositing,
Photography, Consultant**

COMING SOON

THA COME UP

Written by Fleetwood

TO MY FRIEND, MY FAMILY, MY
BROTHA FROM A DIFFERENT
MOTHER WHO LOVES THE SAME
FATHER

RUDY CORPUZ

Director of the UNITED PLAYAZ,
thank you so much for being a solider, a
friend, and my brotha.
I love u dogg.

UNITED PLAYAZ 4 LIFE
believe that

U better ask LightSkin Luther 'bout us
Roscoe…

FREE HARRY O
FREE UNO
BRICKHEAD
BIG KEKE
BENARD
HERBERT
THE LIFERS
AND ALL MY USO'S

ABOUT THE AUTHOR

FLEETWOOD's had a long journey trying to find his destiny. Through his trials and tribulations, he has been molded into the man he is today: a solider in GOD'S war, never claiming to be perfect, but a sinner who loves going to church. Throughout it all he has become a writer, rap artist, music producer, actor, videographer, motivational speaker and com— munity activist. He has an Associate Arts Degree in Music Engineering from Music Tech in Minn— eapolis.

This is Fleetwood's third book. To find out more about Fleetwood, his next book, his com— munity activism, go to www.tagged.com/fleetwood and also facebook.com/Robert Bowden.